Super Hot
Supervisor

USA TODAY BESTSELLING AUTHOR

MANDY HARBIN

Tender Tarts Series

*To my parents for all their words of
encouragement over the years and to my mom
for critiquing many of my earlier stories...
those that did not have sex in them.
Books that weren't like the ones in this series.*

Hey, y'all! There are two points I want to quickly touch on. 1. The publishing industry has changed. 2. Shit happens.

If you follow me on social media, you saw I was a victim of robbery and arson two years ago. At the time, I wrapped up my contractual obligations and then took time to heal. After I finished my crusade of justice and put my big girl panties back on, I turned my attention back to writing and all that entails. Part of that process was taking stock of the contemporary stories I'd published through various means to see if I could package them together.

This series is the result of that effort.

Some of these books were previously published, which I'd gotten the rights back to. Others were only available in limited release. Since I like leaving little nuggets for my readers, some characters crossed over from one series to the other as sort of special-guest appearances. (Pssst...There are even references to characters here from The Bang Shift Series. *wink wink*). Therefore, it made the most sense to repackage them into one, fun, contemporary romance series.

To more fully solidify these interconnected stories, I did some minor rewrites. That being said, you don't have to read the new versions to understand what's going on. Below is a break down of the books previously released, so you can check your e-readers before you choose to buy. I'm working hard on the next Bang Shift Series book, but there are still a couple of fun stories I'd like to add to this rebranded series in the future. ;-)

- **_Super Hot Supervisor_** – Against Company Policy/Digital Possession
- **_California Crush_** – Against the Wall
- **_Hardheaded Hubby_** – Blue Balls and Push-Up Bras
- **_Long Distance Lover_** – Blue Balls and Long Distance Calls
- **_Momma's Boy_** – Blue Balls and Southern Drawls
- **_Billionaire Beefcake_** – Against The Billionaire's Will
- **_Part-Time Player_** – Stripped Dare / Against The Grain

CHAPTER ONE

"Get your ass in gear, girl, we're gonna be late!" Sasha yelled as Cassie was trying to pour a cup of coffee before rushing to the meeting that was suddenly called.

Why was Richard throwing everybody into a tizzy first thing on a Monday morning? Cassie overslept, didn't get her jog in and now was being hustled into a staff meeting. Oh she'd be getting her java first. Richard could kiss it.

"I'm coming," Cassie grumbled, stirring in the creamer as she grabbed her laptop. "What's this about anyway?"

Sasha ran her free hand through her jet-black hair as she juggled her laptop in the other. She was a free spirit, danced to her own tune, which included chopping her hair into a spiky mess and dyeing it, though it suited her spunky persona. "No clue. But I have better things to do than sit in a meeting."

"You and me both," Cassie mumbled as they entered the conference room and took their seats.

"Glad you could join us," Richard said as he pulled down the projection screen for what was probably a video conference. Great. So this wasn't going to be just a staff meeting.

"What's this about?" Sasha asked while she and Cassie logged on to their laptops through the wireless connection in the building.

"You know the application we built for that home security company? Well, the west coast office got a contract to build something similar for a major security company out there. Corporate doesn't want them to reinvent the wheel." He turned to Cassie. "Since you were lead on that project, Tucker, you'll be working with the software development leader in that office to modify the existing application to fit the needs of their client."

Cassie stared at Richard, speechless. The person Richard was talking about was Ian—

"Cope is an efficient leader and will do a fine job on this project," Richard continued, interrupting her thoughts.

Cassie's company-wide IM popped up on her laptop.

Ian Cope is hot as hell! I can't believe you get to work with the west coast hottie.

Apparently, Sasha couldn't wait for the meeting to end before voicing her opinion.

Cassie glanced over at Sasha, but she was covertly arranging her notebook, not looking at Cassie.

"This is Mac. You got us, Richard?" Carl "Mac" Mackenzie asked as he appeared on the screen. He was VP in charge of the west coast office. Cassie didn't care for him much, but she didn't have to deal with him regularly either.

"Yes, Mac. I'll let you drive this meeting."

"Great, thanks. Hi, everyone. Sorry we're just now getting online. I know all of you are busy, but I need to discuss some preliminaries before getting to the heart of the matter."

Mac droned on about quarterly reports while Cassie sipped her coffee and cocked an eyebrow up at Sasha, who was typing.

Who the hell cares about financial statements? It's not like he's addressing corporate.

You know how Mac is, Sasha. I'm just glad we don't work under him, Cassie responded.

Looks like you could be working under Ian Cope. I can think of a lot worse places to be. She threw on a smiley face at the end of her IM.

Wasn't that the truth? Ian Cope was the epitome of masculine yum-yum. With his unruly curly brown hair and light-brown eyes the color of expensive whiskey, he had an attitude just as smooth and intoxicating as the liquor he personified.

Tell me about it, girlfriend. He's a hunk and a half.

At least Cassie didn't have to work with him in person. She hadn't gotten laid in over a year and didn't know how well she'd be able to control herself around such a gorgeous man. The last boyfriend she'd had couldn't deal with her success, but something told her Ian was a very secure man. He was successful too, but he seemed the type to not let money get in the way of what he wanted. Of course she didn't know this for sure, and if she was smart, she would never know. She needed to keep her interaction with him strictly professional. She sat back and sipped her coffee, figuring she should focus on the meeting.

"Cassandra Tucker."

Cassie's head shot up. She coughed, trying not to spit out the brew. Oh shit. They were talking about her.

All heads turned in her direction as she gently placed her cup on the table beside her laptop, dabbing her mouth, and prepared to fake her way through this so as not to embarrass herself further.

Shame on you. Got caught not paying attention.

Cassie read the IM, automatically thinking it was from Sasha. Why would she try to distract her when she should know Cassie needed her wits about her?

It was from Ian, not Sasha.

Double oh shit!

"I think I can take it from here, Mac," Ian volunteered. "As Mac was saying…" He hesitated, throwing a pointed look in Cassie's direction. "We need a prototype built for our client by the tenth of this month. That's next week. I'll be working with Tucker to get it built. It'll be our top priority until it's completed."

"Is this going to cause any problems with your other projects?" Richard asked her.

Cassie straightened in her chair, thankful for Ian's save. "No. I'm finalizing the other large project I'm working on, which is ahead of schedule." She cleared her throat. "Sasha Jones was lead developer on the original build of this application. We could use her team to make the necessary modifications."

"No dice," Mac said suddenly. All eyes turned to him at his outburst. "Cope already has a team in place who's met with our client. They know their needs, and it'll just waste time bringing her team up to speed on the new requirements."

That is bullshit! Sasha messaged to Cassie.

Cassie gave her a sympathetic look. She was right, but from the firm set of Mac's face, it was apparent there'd be no discussion on the matter. Cassie had to tamp down her own irritation.

"Okay, I'll get with Ian Cope this afternoon to get started. If he's available."

"How about two?" he asked.

"Works for me." Cassie didn't look at him, her mind reeling over the implications of this.

"Good. That's all. We'll touch base later on the status," Mac said and disconnected the call after a few courtesy goodbyes.

Cassie stared at Richard because Sasha looked as if she were about to blow a gasket, and Cassie wasn't that far behind either. "What the hell's going on? Why is Mac acting holier than thou, not letting Sasha's team in on this?"

Richard raised his hands in a placating gesture. "Don't take it out on me. I have no idea why they don't want to use her team." He looked at Sasha and shrugged.

"Well, it seems to me if they didn't want to reinvent the wheel, then they'd use the same developers who coded the application," Sasha spat.

Cassie shook her head and sighed, reining in her anger. "Sasha, everything is in the data library. They can pull the work that was done and use it. I have a feeling they've already done that."

Richard's cheeks tinged red and he

looked down. It was evident that was exactly what had happened.

"Oh my God! Why didn't you give us a heads-up?" Sasha demanded.

"It was out of my hands." He sounded defeated, so there really was no reason in berating him over this.

"C'mon, Sasha. You can help me go over the coding, so at least I'm prepared for my meeting this afternoon."

Cassie grabbed Sasha's arm and hauled her out of the conference room and to her cubicle.

"This is such bullshit!" Sasha whispered as she put her laptop on her docking station and booted it back up.

"I know. But I need you to focus. I've already been caught sitting down on the job."

"Oh please. No one knew you were distracted, chatting with me during the meeting." Sasha waved her hand dismissively.

"Not true. Ian sent me an IM. He wanted it known that he, at least, caught me, so now I have to make sure I do a really great job on this."

Sasha's eyes got wide, then narrowed. "You tell that hunk of man to kiss your ass. I don't care how sexy he is. Don't let him bully you on this project."

"Oh I won't, but since Weiner threw me to the wolves wrapped in raw meat, I want to make sure I'm prepared for my next encounter."

Sasha chuckled. "Now why in the hell does Richard Weiner call everyone by their last names when he was cursed with the one he got? I mean, really? Dick Weiner? I'd cut my dad's pecker off in his sleep if he named me that!"

Cassie laughed with Sasha, and it eased the tension of the morning. Now Cassie had to focus. She had a new project, and she damn sure was going to do a good job.

———

IAN COPE WAS FINALLY GETTING what he'd wished for—a chance to work with Cassie Tucker. When Mac had told him they'd be pulling her in on this project, Ian had covered his excitement. He'd had a thing for her for the past two years, waiting for the right opportunity to work with her while dropping subtle hints to his boss whenever an opportunity presented itself. Mac had finally listened, but she didn't seem too thrilled to be working on this project for some reason. Her disgruntled face as the conference call ended was a blow to the ol' ego, but Ian could work with that. He just had to play this very carefully.

"Come with me to my office, Cope," Mac said.

Ian nodded as he gathered his laptop and meeting book, then followed his boss.

"What's up?"

"Shut the door and take a seat."

Ian suppressed a sigh. He had work to do, and that included figuring out how to woo his new coworker. But he followed the orders and waited for Mac to speak his mind.

"There's a reason why we've pulled the south regional office in on this project."

"Yeah, I know they've already built a similar project and I've already started looking at it. It's really close to what we need for our new client."

"Cope, the game is changing. Corporate wants us to make a move into the security industry. If we can generalize this software and promote it to that sector, we could push our company to the forefront of our competitors and corner the market."

"And you want to do this with the application they've already built."

Mac chuckled. "Not exactly. See, I know you could've built a customizable application that'd fit our client's needs and the bigwigs' desire to initiate their strategy. The deal is that they also want to cut costs. We are looking at closing the south regional office."

Ian stared at Mac, not sure what to say. Why would corporate want to do that?

"Someone has to go. We just got that major contract, so we're in the clear. That office is the smartest choice to be cut. The fact this project came up gave us an in."

Ian felt his blood boiling. "An in to what?" he asked.

"I need you to prepare a consolidation plan on their outstanding projects, showing how their work can be absorbed by other associates within the company at other locations. Cassandra Tucker is high enough up in the company that you should be able to get all the information you need from her under the guise of this project."

Ian shot to his feet. "You want me to lie to her?" he asked incredulously.

Mac's face turned venomous. "Well, now. You've been champing at the bit to work with little Miss Tucker. So here's your chance. Get to know her. Get to know everything about that office. And do it without her finding out why. As of now, she's already out of a job. Don't lose yours too."

CHAPTER TWO

CASSIE ATE lunch at her desk so she could read over the coding on the application her office had built for the local home security company in preparation for her meeting with Ian. She hardly ate, though. She dug herself into her work because she wanted to make a good impression. She'd never worked with him in the past, so she felt as if she had something to prove. Her track record was impeccable, but it wasn't as if she could pull out all her old projects and gloat about what she was capable of. She had to show him on this project.

But why did her thoughts wander to inappropriate things? Things like how his touch would feel when he caressed her cheek with his barely calloused hands. He wouldn't have rough hands since he didn't do manual labor, but they wouldn't be really soft either. He was the type of man who didn't mind getting his hands dirty doing his own work around the house. And because his hands would show signs of work, so would his chest, his biceps. He'd be able to hold her down, keep her still while she tried to writhe as her orgasm built from him licking her pussy.

Cassie felt flush just thinking about what he could do with his tongue, hands, body. God, she needed to get laid something fierce! She was a professional, for crying out loud.

Her company cell phone buzzed, startling her with the signal she had a new text message.

Stuck in another meeting. Need to push ours back thirty minutes.

Ian. If he only knew what she'd been thinking about. Her heart raced, which was silly. It wasn't as if he were some guy sending her a personal text. This was business. She should use that extra half-hour reprieve to screw her head back on straight.

No problem, she responded.

Really sorry if this messes up your schedule.

Hmm. She didn't think he'd respond again. What should she say? *It's okay. Just let me know when you're ready.* There. That was professional enough. Now he could get back to his meeting and she could try to keep her mind out of the gutter.

I'm ready now but can't get away from these goons.

Cassie smiled. Ian was texting her, chatting with her. Her palms started sweating. She knew this was business, but she could pretend for a minute he was just a hot guy texting her.

Shame on you, not paying attention to your meeting. She chuckled as she sent that message to him.

LOL! Didn't take you long to use my words against me.

What can I say? I'm good.

After a couple of minutes with no response, Cassie shook her head with a smile as she tossed her phone onto her desk. Time to get back to work. She logged back into her laptop as her phone buzzed again.

I intend to find out.

Was she on a roller coaster? Because her stomach just dropped. Surely he was just talking about finding out how good she was at her job. That was what he had to have meant.

We're finishing up now. I'll be online in ten minutes.

God, she was an idiot. Of course that was all he had meant. She quickly typed a confirmation and gathered her notes for their meeting. When she logged into the webinar, he was already there.

Time to put her game face on. They had a job to do and she wanted him to be impressed by her. Fantasies would have to wait for after-hours.

———

IAN WAITED for Cassie to log on to their meeting, reading over their texts. He didn't know if he wanted the innuendo to be blatantly obvious or for her to be oblivious to his come-on. God, he was in another state. It wasn't as if anything could come of this. Especially not now that Mac had him doing his dirty work. Yeah, Ian was in a meeting earlier, but what he'd found out was that Mac was the one who was supposed to devise a migration plan for the closure of the south regional office. But when this project started, it was his way to pawn off the work to Ian.

Now Ian was stuck. He'd waited and practically begged to work with Cassie for two years. Well, he got exactly what he wanted. He had to get close enough to her to get her talking about work not specific to their project. He hated lying to her, and he knew even if she was interested in him, he couldn't forge a relationship on a lie. He needed to cool it, get this project finished, and maybe then he could look her up. Maybe he should friend her on Facebook. It'd provide an opening to her afterward since all their interactions so far had been through company means. He'd then be able to lend a sympathetic ear to the atrocities of corporate cutbacks and even help her find a new job.

When she logged on to the meeting, he

sighed. God, she was beautiful. Brown hair and light-green eyes. Her brown suit and tan blouse would probably look bland on anyone else, but it complemented her creamy skin tone, making it look as if it were bathed in milk. He needed to snap out of it and get this ball rolling.

"Hey there, sorry for the delay. I copied the application and loaded it into a development environment. I'm sending you the path now."

"Great."

"I'm also sending you the notes I have on what our client wants. I've already noted some changes, but since you're more familiar with this application, you might be able to tell me where best to modify it."

"Okay. I'll read over that tonight."

Ian shook his head and adjusted his earphones. "No, no. I don't want you working after-hours on this. We should be able to finish without any overtime."

Cassie laughed, and Ian could swear he felt her breath on his neck. He stifled a groan when his cock twitched.

"I don't mind. Really."

"Well, if you are, then I am."

She laughed again, the sound that of an angel. Fuck! What was wrong with him?

"You must not have a life either," she said, still chuckling as she jotted down something in her notebook.

"Married to my job."

"Same here."

Ian felt a pang of sadness. She was dedicated to a job she was about to lose. He was such a piece of shit for not giving her a heads-up.

But there wasn't anything he could do, so he needed to use this opportunity to start his investigation.

"You got a lot of projects going on?"

"Not too many. How about you?"

Crap. Her answer was not only too vague, but she threw his question right back at him. Maybe if he was specific, she'd be too.

"I lead three projects that are long-term and handle smaller ones as they come up. You?"

"Wow. No wonder you stay busy. I don't have anything going on long-term. When I'm in the last leg of a project, my time gets scheduled on whatever's up next. Sometimes they overlap, but I've never worked on more than three major projects at the same time."

"I'm jealous." Ian chuckled. "No wonder you produce good work—you're not frazzled out from being stretched too thin."

Cassie smiled softly and Ian had to clench his fist to keep from stroking the monitor like a moron.

"Why, thank you." Her Southern drawl was thicker than it had been, and it was quite possibly the most adorable thing he'd ever heard. "But it is how things are done here. Everyone is assigned projects based on their area of expertise, and we work in teams to complete them on schedule. Even if I'm not assigned to a particular project, I'm known to jump in and help when I think I have something to contribute."

He smiled and leaned closer to the monitor. "I wish everyone was like that. It'd make my job a lot easier."

Her head fell back as she laughed carelessly. Even the column of her neck looked inviting. He'd give anything to collar it. No, he wasn't a Dom, but he knew he had some dominant tendencies that flared to life every now and then.

Like right now.

"Then I wouldn't be special."

"Nothing would change how special you are," Ian said huskily.

Cassie gasped, her eyes boring into the screen.

Fuck! Why did he say that? He cleared his throat. "Um, I think we've got enough to go on for now. How about we meet back up in the morning and compare notes?"

"Er, okay."

"Great," he said quickly. "Talk to you later."

"Bye."

He disconnected the meeting, yanked his earphones off and threw them on his desk.

What the hell had gotten into him? Had he not just told himself to cool it where she was concerned because nothing could come of this? Not right now, anyway? Jesus! He was acting like a sixteen-year-old with his first girlfriend. Next thing he knew, he'd be having wet dreams at the thought of just copping a feel.

He ran his hands through his disheveled hair, realizing he had to get out of here. He logged off and grabbed his laptop, thinking over the rest of their meeting as he bolted. At least he did learn a little about the dynamics of her office. It didn't seem as if she was juggling too many projects, and the way she talked, that was the norm for everyone there. It was a start.

A start to his betrayal of her. Fuck! He needed a beer.

CHAPTER THREE

CASSIE WAS SNUGGLED in her pj's, sitting on her bed with her laptop while she worked. So what if she was on her second glass of wine? She needed the help relaxing her nerves after her meeting with Ian. Damn, but the man was sex on a stick and she'd love to eat him up. What had he meant about calling her special? That comment was so out of the blue, and she could tell that it caught him off guard too.

Great. There she went again, getting distracted. She downed the rest of her glass and filled it back up. She'd had enough of work, anyway. Ian got a good start and was definitely on the right track where the changes needed to be made. She documented some other areas where modifications were needed and emailed everything to Ian. Now she wanted to chat with Sasha to get her perspective on what happened today, and if she knew her good friend, she'd be online playing Farmville by now. The woman loved that game. Even after everyone got over it and started on the next big craze, Sasha had remained faithful to it. Oh, she played other games, too, but that was her favorite by far. Yeah, she didn't have a life either. She just didn't spend her free time working.

Cassie logged on and saw that Sasha was too, just as she'd figured.

Quit playing Farmville so we can chat! Cassie messaged her.

LOL! You know me so well. What's up?

Cassie relayed her meeting with Ian in short messages that Sasha quickly responded to.

Holy shit! Methinks he has the hots for you.

Methinks you're crazy. He couldn't end the meeting fast enough after that slip.

So you think he was just distracted and didn't realize what he was saying?

Cassie sighed as she sipped more wine. She didn't know what to think. That was why she told Sasha. *I need an unbiased opinion on what I should do.*

Girl, you need to tell Dick Weiner that you need to fly out to the west coast office to work one-on-one with Ian.

Cassie laughed as she gulped more wine. *Shut up! I'm not doing that. I need help staying focused on my job, not help plotting ways to seduce the west coast hottie.*

You're no fun. Okay, fine. Quit fantasizing about him.

Ugh! I need reasons why.

Hmmm. How about, you don't know him. He could live at home with his momma.

Cassie laughed and nodded. *That's good. I need more, though.*

What could be worse than a titty baby? Okay. You've only ever seen him from the waist up. He could be five-two. Oh, wait. His dick could be broken. You've never even seen a cock bulge.

Cassie snorted and almost spat out her wine. *A short titty baby with a broken dick. Only you could come up with that.*

I aim to please, sister. Hold on a sec while I check my crops.

Good Lord. Sasha was a Farmville junkie. Cassie used the opportunity to check her messages and new friend requests. She ignored the ones she didn't recognize and accepted a few old classmates from high school.

She nearly dropped her glass when she saw her request from Ian Cope. No way. She hadn't checked her Facebook account in almost a week, but this had to have been recent.

Okay, I'm back, Sasha messaged.

You'll never guess who sent me a friend request.

Not Paul from accounting again? Just ignore it. He'll get the picture eventually.

Er, no. Ian.

Well, well, Mr. Short Titty Baby may have a broken cock, but he sure as hell has balls. You accept it?

Not yet.

Whatcha waiting for? He might have nekkid pics of himself on his page.

Cassie sighed. What was she waiting for? It wasn't as if she hadn't accepted friend requests from others she worked with. She quickly accepted it before she could give it any more thought.

Just did.

Good girl.

Either Cassie was starting to feel the effects of all this yummy wine she'd downed so far or she was lightheaded from what just happened. She preferred to put the blame on the alcohol. She was getting ready to respond when a new message window popped up.

Hi. You're up late.

Shiiiiiit!

Gotta go, Sasha. Ian just messaged me.

Get out! Girl, I want deets on the morrow.

She closed their chat and stared at Ian's message. What the hell was she going to say? Guess honesty was the way to go.

Was working. You have some great ideas. I sent you some other changes that I think need to be made.

Good. You have a Skype account? Since you're working anyway, we can meet right now and go over some things without being interrupted.

Er, no, she didn't have a Skype account. Her family lived close by and the only people she talked to online like that were through work.

Nope. But I can sign up real quick. I'm sure it's not rocket science.

I'll log on. Just do a search for my name and add me as a contact. Then select me and click video call.

Cassie created an account and added him as he'd requested. It was really easy. She opened up another window and logged on to her work network through the VPN connection, so she'd be ready for their impromptu meeting. Then she clicked the appropriate button on Skype to initiate the call.

"Hi, there," Ian said when he came into view.

God, he was gorgeous. Cassie had only seen him in a tie, unless he wore a polo on casual days. Now he was in a tight-fitting t-shirt. It was faded but showed some football team and fit him like a second skin. He sat far enough back from his computer that she could see the tops of his lounge pants and upper thighs, but was too far for her to notice any bulge to discredit Sasha's silly broken-dick theory.

He took a swig of his beer and set it aside, his muscles rippling with little effort. When he licked his lips, moisture pooled between her legs. She fantasized about what he could do with that wet tongue. Her nipples hardened, making her acutely aware of how thin her spaghetti-strap top was. She suddenly realized she'd had way too much to drink tonight and shouldn't have agreed to this, but was too buzzed to care as much as she should.

"Hey," she said a little too breathlessly, grabbing her glass of wine, swallowing the last of it and filling it up again, damn near draining the bottle. With as much as she'd had to drink, her mouth shouldn't be so dry.

He chuckled. "Looks like you've had fun tonight. Unless you had someone helping you with that bottle." He took another pull of his beer.

"Nope. And I actually stopped working before I really started feeling the effects, just so you know."

He threw his hands up, one still holding his beer. "Oh hey, I'm not here to judge. I'm on my fourth one of these."

"Good, then if I go down, I'm taking you with me." She chuckled as she took another sip.

Something dark flashed across Ian's eyes but was gone before she could fully analyze it. "So tell me about yourself, Cope."

He cocked an eyebrow with his beer

halfway to his luscious mouth. "What do you want to know, Tucker?"

She tilted her head as she thought. "Do you live at home with your mom?" Cassie blurted.

He spewed beer before throwing his hand up to his mouth. He swallowed and coughed as he laughed. "Where the hell did that come from?"

She was trying not to laugh at the scene he made, but she wasn't doing a very good job. "Just answer the question, Cope," she said with mock seriousness.

"No, I don't live with my mom."

"Damn," Cassie muttered as she took another sip of her wine. *There goes one possible theory.*

"What did you say?"

"Oh nothing, nothing." She waved her hands dismissively. "I probably should've just asked how tall you were instead."

"What does that have to do with living with my mom?" There was genuine amusement in his eyes.

Cassie shrugged innocently. It wasn't as if she could come out and tell him about her conversation with Sasha.

"I'm six-two."

"Damn!" she mumbled into her wineglass.

He laughed. "I don't know if I should be offended or what. Normally, women like a tall man who doesn't live at home with mommy."

"Not me."

Ian leaned forward, setting his beer down. "No?"

"No. I like short titty babies all the way. Even better if they have broken dicks."

He threw his head back in a fit of laughter and slapped his chest, leaving his hand over his heart while he got his composure. Damn, but he was sexy. Cassie wished she could just crawl through the screen and straddle his lap.

"Well, I'm batting zero, darlin'," he said as he wiped his eyes.

"I knew it'd never work," she said, feigning disappointment.

His smile began to fade and he swallowed, though he didn't take a drink. He rubbed his hands on what had to be his legs, but Cassie couldn't see that far. He seemed to be getting uncomfortable, and she felt guilty for allowing the conversation to trickle into an inappropriate area. Heat tinged her cheeks, but as much as she wanted to say it was because of embarrassment, she knew that'd be a lie. No matter how he felt, she was turned-on and too buzzed to be smart about this. Her pussy was wet and she ached to touch it. Oh yeah, as soon as she ended this call, she'd be taking care of herself, pretending it was Ian Cope.

She finished her wine quickly. "Well, I think I'm too drunk to get any work done." And too horny. "I'll catch you tomorrow."

"Wait, I—"

"Bye."

Cassie clicked the button and the screen got smaller. Then she pushed her laptop away and fell back on her bed. God, why did that man have to be the hottest thing she'd even seen? And now she knew he was tall, self-sufficient with a working dick. She groaned at the thought of what he could do with his big, hard cock and pushed her pants and panties down her thighs. She let her fingers trail lightly over her belly to her pussy, slowly tracing the seam.

"I want you to touch me," she whispered, imagining it was Ian's finger about to breach her barrier.

Her finger slipped into her wet folds and she gasped. She pushed two fingers inside and fucked herself slowly, teasingly. She worked her fingers, thrusting until more cream flooded her. Then she pulled out, circling her swollen nub.

"Yes," she breathed. "Like that."

She wanted Ian's mouth on her, ravishing her, drinking her honey, sucking her clit, his large body hovering over her, dominating her. Even though she tried it once, she never really got into the whole Dom/sub dynamic, but she had to admit a little domination was sexy as hell. Just the thought of him holding her down, seeing to her pleasure, ensuring his own, was enough to send her to the edge. She stopped teasing herself and shoved her fingers back inside her pussy while she used her other hand to rub her clit. She frantically tried to get herself off, thrusting her hips up, fucking herself while she fingered her hard button. She was moaning, so close, almost there.

She squeezed her eyes shut because she started to see stars. Then colors exploded behind her eyelids as her climax hit. She was panting as she brought herself down from the heights of her pleasure when she heard a masculine roar. She shot up in the bed, yanking herself out of her foggy bliss to see Ian's image within a smaller screen on the laptop. *Oh, fuck! Please don't be a live shot.* She clicked to enlarge it and gasped when she saw him sitting in the same place he'd been when she had disconnected their video call—or when she'd thought she'd disconnected it.

Only he wasn't watching her. His head was thrown back, his hand fisted around his cock, stroking it while cum shot onto his belly and all over his hand.

She was frozen as she stared, mortified at what he'd witnessed, yet fascinated at what he was doing.

Groaning, he looked up and saw her looking at him, her image sobering him.

"Cassie, I—"

She shut the laptop before he could finish.

This was bad. This was very bad.

CHAPTER FOUR

CASSIE WASN'T ANSWERING her cell the next morning, and when Ian tried calling her office line, he got her voicemail. He sent her an email but got an out-of-office reply stating she was out for the day.

He wanted to talk to her and was irritated she was obviously avoiding him, but what the hell was he going to say when he finally reached her? *Sorry I invaded your privacy with my voyeuristic kinks?* Yeah, that'd go over really well. He felt like the biggest asshole on the planet. He knew she'd tried to end the connection last night, so he should have done it for her. But it happened so fast there was a small part of him hoping her actions were on purpose, and if there was the slightest chance that was the case, he wasn't going to stop the show.

Damn, but the woman was beautiful, and the sexiest little vixen he'd ever laid eyes on.

If he had any doubts about her attraction to him, last night quashed them. Granted she was drunk, but she had to be thinking about him when she got off since she'd yanked her panties down inside of five seconds after talking to him.

And after Ian got over the shock of seeing Cassie masturbate, he couldn't not touch himself too. He'd already been hard as steel from her flirting banter. He'd had every intention of jacking off last night anyway, but watching her touch herself caused his hard cock to ache beyond any sanity he could've clung to. He'd pulled out his dick before he'd even realized what he was doing. All logic flew right out the window, right along with his morals.

And here he was trying to pin his actions on the hope that she'd meant for him to watch. Yeah, he was definitely a first-rate asshole.

Ian spent the morning going over the changes that Cassie had sent him last night. She'd done a really great job understanding the requirements and identifying areas where the changes could be made to best meet the client's needs. He also noted some modifications to build a generalized prototype pursuant to his instructions that trickled down from corporate. He met with his development team to initiate the work and set a timeline to complete it in two days. He'd work on the test plan documentation to get it ready for testing, and in the meantime, he would hope that two days would give Cassie enough time to muster up the courage to face his sorry ass.

The least he could do was cover for her calling in.

Then again, it wasn't as if she would have a job for much longer anyway. He shouldn't worry how it looked.

But he did. He'd liked her for too long, and he had always known his interest was more than just a physical attraction. He respected her professionally too, and the last thing he wanted was for her to look bad.

Especially since he was the reason.

Ian left the meeting with his developers and ran right into his boss.

"How's everything coming along, Cope?"

"Good, Mac. Just finished meeting with the development team on the changes that are needed."

Mac glanced around, making Ian do the same. "Have you gotten anything from Tucker?" he asked in a hushed tone, so he obviously wasn't asking about the official project.

"Yes sir. I'm learning about the inner workings of her office. I should have something for you next week."

"Just make sure you wrap up the consolidation plan by the time your project is finished."

Ian did his best to seem nonchalant. He knew it wouldn't do to come across as a prick right now, no matter how much he hated what he was being forced to do.

"I'll get it done," he said curtly and stalked off.

He had no choice but to do the job assigned to him. He'd just have to get back in Cassie's good graces first.

And he'd have to shove all his fantasies about her into the deepest, darkest recesses of his brain. Because if he dwelled on the things he still wanted to do to her, he'd be in some serious trouble.

Trouble he yearned for.

———

"YOU FIDDLED the bean in front of Ian?" Sasha yelled loud enough that Cassie had to pull her phone away from her ear.

"Of course you'd focus on the details." Cassie sighed as she flung herself onto the bed and threw the covers over her head. She didn't think she could get any more embarrassed after last night. She was quickly finding out that wasn't the case. Having to relive the experience was almost just as bad. Almost.

"I told you I wanted deets."

"You got deets. Now I need help," Cassie groaned.

Sasha sighed. "Cass, listen. You need to just chill. So you two got a little freaky last night. You're consenting adults. You're entitled."

"But I didn't know! It's hard to say I was consenting when I didn't exactly get to consent."

"Good grief, girl. You practically shoved your pussy in his face. You can't get much more consenting than that." When Cassie didn't respond, Sasha continued. "I get why you're upset but just try and think about what he's going through too. You both were hitting the sauce and getting cozy in your pj's. If he'd actually been at your place, you would've fucked."

"You don't know that!"

"Whatever. Stay in denial. The bottom line is you have to work with him. You can't avoid him forever. You're on a tight schedule on this project, Cass."

"Yeah, yeah, I know. And he tried calling me several times today. I checked my email, and not only did he try getting me to talk to him that way, but he actually got the ball rolling on our project and kept me up to speed on what he'd done. I don't want him covering my ass."

"I bet he could cover it quite nicely right after he pulls his cock out—"

"Sasha!"

Unfortunately, Cassie's reprimand only furthered Sasha's laughter.

"Okay, all right, okay. But you have to admit you're being a little petty. He probably feels terrible and maybe even a little creepy. There's no telling what's going through his mind, and you're not giving him an opportunity to talk about what happened."

Cassie really hated that Sasha was being logical. But how could Cassie face Ian now? It wasn't as if she carefully orchestrated a seduction to pull him in with a sultry feminine show meant to fire him up. Nope, she just dropped her drawers and went at it. No teasing, tempting play. And working a man up into a frenzy was the best part. Well, one of the best parts. Cassie loved it when a man lost control and exerted his carnal, basic instincts. She didn't want a knuckle-dragging Neanderthal, but there was something to be said for a man's primitive reaction to a woman. The fact that Ian didn't hold back was sexy as hell.

And how could she tell him she was both embarrassed and turned-on by what had happened? He'd think she was a total freak. A total *flaky* freak who didn't know what she wanted.

"I know you're right, Sasha. I'm going to eat some dinner and then respond to his email about the project. I'd rather touch base tonight than tomorrow."

"Good idea. Let me know how it goes."

Cassie rang off and ordered pizza while she read over the work Ian had done and contemplated her response. After the pizza arrived and she gorged herself on yummy pepperoni goodness, she took the bull by the horns and sent him a response, mentioning how great of a job he had done and that she'd get started on the white paper tomorrow since he was tackling the test plan. She was in the middle of talking herself into taking a much-needed shower—she'd skipped one this morning because she was too hungover to get out of bed—when her phone rang. She grabbed the receiver and sighed when she saw Ian's name. His emails were sent to his BlackBerry, so he'd have known she was working. It wasn't as if she could keep avoiding him. Besides, she'd rather have this conversation away from the prying ears lurking around cubicle land.

"Hello." She was proud of how relaxed she actually sounded.

"Hi, Cassie. It's Ian. I think it's a great idea to get started on the white paper. I hadn't actually thought about that yet." He sounded like his regular, professional self, and she felt a little more at ease. "I, er, talked to the lead developer again after I sent you the status update, and he seems pretty confident that it'll be ready for us to test in a couple of days."

"Good."

Uncomfortable silence. One second turned into two, three, four.

"I'm sorry," he breathed.

Cassie shut her eyes. His tone was beyond apologetic. It was tortured.

"It's not your fault, Ian. If I was too drunk to realize I hadn't disconnected our call, then you deserved the little show you got." She shook her head, playing with the imaginary lint on her pajama bottoms.

"No. I took advantage of the situation. That was not cool. I-I...shit, Cassie," he sighed, and she could imagine he looked just as frustrated as he sounded. "I knew it was wrong, but I couldn't stop myself. The thing is I told myself you might've known I was watching and you were doing it on purpose. Granted it was a very, very small part of me that had hoped that while the rest of me was screaming to disconnect, but if there was even the slightest possibility you wanted me with you when you...then I wanted to share it with you," he whispered the last part.

He wanted to share it with her? Not just get off too? What was he saying?

"Look, we'd both been drinking—"

"I'd have done that with you cold-stone sober. Seeing your beautiful body was a very sobering experience anyway."

How she could manage to blush from his words after what had happened last night, she didn't understand, but that was definitely happening. Her face felt inflamed, and her hands started trembling. There was no way the west coast hottie could think she was beautiful. Sure, she'd had her fair share of admirers and felt pretty good about her looks. But feeling pretty good about looks was a far cry from thinking she could turn this sex god's head when his sobriety wasn't in question.

So why was she melting, slinking onto the bed with thoughts of what that hunk of man could do to her? She shouldn't encourage this. She really shouldn't...

"Is that so?" she breathed. So much for being smart about this.

A low groan filtered through the phone. "God, yes."

"Yes, you'd have done that anyway, or yes, you think I'm beautiful?"

"Both," he answered without hesitation.

She didn't want to focus on the comment about her looks. She felt as if she'd be fishing for compliments if she asked him to explain. Besides, he could just be flattering her to ease his conscience. But she could definitely get the skinny on the other. "So you've had internet sex before?" She laughed at the thought of what they'd essentially done.

He chuckled. "Actually, I can't say that I have."

"Oh, we were both internet sex virgins, then."

He laughed louder. "I haven't been an anything virgin in a long time."

"So you've done everything else already?" Cassie couldn't seem to pull her decorum back from the gutter from where she'd dumped it.

"Define 'everything else'," he said cautiously.

"Oh no, my response might show too much of my dark side before I'm ready." Plus he might think she was weak if she told him about the experience that came to mind—the time she submitted sexually to a man. It wasn't a way of life for her, but it sure was fun to try, an experience she'd loved that she would be willing to do again with the right man. "How 'bout you tell me the kinkiest thing you've done."

"Hmmm. You want me to show my cards before you do," he said playfully, then hesitated and cleared his throat. "Dark side, huh? All right. I went to a sex club in L.A. with my brother, Aaron." Was he a damn mind reader? When she didn't say anything right away, he continued. "He's a Dom, and I have some dominant...urges, I guess you can say. It's not a lifestyle choice I could make, but Aaron, he's the real deal. Doesn't like 'weak-ass men', as he puts it, coming in and pretending to be a Dom, so he doesn't usually entertain inquiries into that life. But when I expressed an interest, he showed me around, gave me a taste of it. I know more now about what I like and what I don't. He thinks people who dabble in it and don't invest fully into the life give it a bad rap. I disagree. I think there's no harm in playing a little without the major commitment." He sighed. "And I probably just freaked you the hell out."

Oh, she wasn't freaked out. Not at all. Just hearing Ian talk about being dominant in bed got her hot as hell. "No," she said a little breathlessly.

"Well, now, if I didn't scare you off with that little tale, you must have a little kink in you. Ready to show your cards now? What's the craziest thing you've done?"

She turned to her side, glancing at her reflection in the mirror across the room. She didn't realize her eyes were glazed over, though she should've known. Her pussy was drenched and her nipples were aching. Ian was a dream man, and not only were his looks off the chart, but the two of them also liked the same things in the sack. This was so unfair! Why did this man have to live in another state? If he were here right now, there'd be a lot less talking and a lot more fucking going on. "I know this is going to sound completely ironic, but I swear what I'm about to say is the exact thing that popped into my mind when I asked you that question." Oh God, she was really going to tell him! She'd never told anyone about this. Until now. "I've, er, yeah, I've submitted sexually to a man before."

She heard his sudden intake of breath and her heart raced at his reaction. She wasn't the only one turned-on. The image of him stroking his dick came to mind and she suppressed a moan. Damn, but that had been a sexy sight to see last night.

She wanted to see it again.

"What happened when you submitted?" he rasped.

"I, um, he blindfolded me, chained me to the wall and kissed me...with his crop."

"Fuck," he breathed. "How long did he beat you?"

Her laugh was but a sultry little sound. "Awhile. Until my ass was on fire. Then he fucked me while I was still manacled."

"God, Cassie, was that what you wanted?"

"That question is one of concern, but your tone betrays you," she chided playfully. "You liked hearing about my experience."

He groaned. "Damn, baby. Like doesn't even begin to describe it." At least he was honest with her. After hearing about his dominant tendencies, she knew he'd enjoy hearing her story. "But you didn't answer the question."

"Did I like it? Well, yeah, Ian. I wouldn't have agreed to it if I didn't. But honestly, I'm not a masochist. I got off on the experience because he got off doing it."

"So you wouldn't want to be beaten just for your own pleasure."

"No. Now that doesn't mean I wouldn't find pleasure in it, because I know I have before. But I wouldn't wake up one morning and ask some guy to whip me with a crop for the hell of it."

He made a noncommittal noise as if he was digesting this information, filing it away for future study. He was learning stuff about her that no one else knew. But Cassie didn't want to be the only one spilling the beans tonight.

"What did you do at the sex club, Ian? Did you spank some pretty, young thing?"

"Yes." His voice was ragged with need. "Would you let me spank you while I fucked you?"

She gasped at his raw desire. God, would she ever! Her legs fell open, her hand splaying on her exposed belly. "Oh yeah. I'd let you, and I'd love the feel of your hand on my bare ass."

"Damn, baby, you have a dirty little mouth on you. I'd have given anything to be able to hear the whispered words you said last night while you touched yourself."

"Mmmm..." Her fingers lightly traced her bellybutton.

"Where are you at right now?"

"In bed," she said slowly.

"Good." He took a deep breath. "Take you shirt off, Cassie," he ordered, his tone brooking no argument.

"Why? You can't see my breasts."

"Because I want them exposed. Do it now." He said it with such finality that Cassie sat up in the bed. He was giving her a taste of his dominant nature.

And she was more than eager to sample it.

CHAPTER FIVE

IAN SAT ON HIS BED, leaning against his pillows with the phone propped against his shoulder. He'd never had internet sex before last night, and now it seemed he'd be having phone sex for the first time too. He wasn't some wet-behind-the-ears guy when it came to matters of lust. Truth was he'd had plenty of sex in his life. Good, dirty, sweaty sex in a multitude of positions and sometimes with as many partners who could fit on a king-size bed. He liked it rough. He liked it sweet. He just liked what he liked and wasn't too picky about trying new things.

And because he liked exploring the boundaries of his sexuality, he'd tried that one time being a full Dom. It wasn't for him. He liked being controlling in the bedroom. Hell, he loved that shit! But he also liked it when a woman exerted a little control. And he did not like the idea of dominating a woman outside the bedroom. Having a woman who'd kneel naked at his feet while he ate dinner with his buddies did absolutely zero for his libido. And zero for his ego. His brother, Aaron, on the other hand... Man, that guy was in it to win it. It just wasn't Ian's cup of tea.

But exerting control over a woman sexually from time to time? Yeah, that got the blood flowing to his cock.

Like right fucking now. His dick was harder than steel just thinking about Cassie submitting to him. And not that prick she was talking about. The thought of her submitting to any man other than him made him see red. He'd kill any motherfucker who tried to control her. But God, the thought of him tying her up and ordering her to do his bidding... He shivered. His hands shook. And his cock? It was pressed against the zipper of his jeans, demanding attention.

"Hold on," Cassie said, and he took that time to alleviate his discomfort by easing the zipper down and releasing his aching erection. He pulled it out and suppressed a groan when he gently stroked it. He wanted her soft hands on him instead. "Okay. I took it off."

"Good girl. Now tell me what your nipples look like."

"They're small and pink." She gasped and he felt the jolt in his balls. She was playing with them already.

"Did I say you could touch them?"

"No," she said with the sexiest little pout in her voice.

"You're being a bad girl now, Cassie. Don't do anything unless you're told."

She whimpered. "All right."

"What are you wearing?"

"My pajama bottoms and panties."

"The same bottoms you had on last night?"

"Yeah," she breathed.

Ian could almost picture her lush breasts exposed, her wavy brown hair tumbled around her head, and her light-green eyes half-lidded. She was a fucking bombshell, and she didn't even act like it, which made her even sexier. "Push your pj's and panties down to your knees like you did last night."

He heard her rustle around on her bed while he caressed his cock, stoking his own pleasure with his hand while Cassie did it with her responses.

"Okay. Are you undressing too?"

"I haven't, but I have my pants undone and my hand around my dick. Do you want me to undress, Cassie?"

"Just your shirt."

He smiled. If he took off his shirt, they'd

both be dressed the same. Or undressed the same, actually. "Give me a sec." He put the phone down long enough to pull his shirt off. He tossed it to the side, then picked up the phone again. "Okay. Can you lick your nipples?"

"I-I don't know. I've never tried."

"Try now."

She panted into the phone and moaned with a wet licking sound. "Yeah, I can."

"That's good, Cassie." His balls were already tingling and his belly burning with the need for release. He had to slow down or he'd blow way before he wanted to. "Lick your middle finger and circle your hard little clit for me, baby."

She gasped and a few seconds later groaned into the phone. "Ian," she breathed.

Holy shit, hearing her moaning his name almost undid him. He stroked his dick faster. "That's it, baby. Tease that pretty little nub. Does that feel good?"

"Yeah. It's hot and wet. I wish you could fuck me."

"Shit, Cassie. I'd hold you down and drive my cock so far in you that you wouldn't be able to tell where I stopped and you began. Do you want that? Do you think you could take this big, hard cock?"

"God, yes! Let me touch my clit," she begged.

"Not yet, baby. I want you to shove two fingers inside that sweet pussy."

She cried out and he had to squeeze his dick to keep from coming. "Fuck yourself with those fingers, baby."

"Ian, I'm getting close. I want you to come with me."

"Oh yeah. How do you want me to come?"

She hesitated, and he could hear her shallow intakes of breath. He'd give anything to be hovered over her right now, poised to ram his dick into her so fast she'd arch off the bed and force him deeper into her drenched pussy.

"I-I want you to spit into your hand, shut your eyes and visualize my mouth around your cock."

He groaned, sweat beading on his brow. Damn, he'd love to have those plump lips wrapped around his dick, sucking him off. He pulled his hand away, spitting into it as she requested, and wrapped it around his cock again. "Ahhh, yes, baby," he whispered, leaning his head back and shutting his eyes, letting his mind create the image of her head between his legs. "Rub your clit with your other hand while you continue to fuck your-self with those greedy little fingers."

She panted and he squeezed his eyes shut tighter, gritting his teeth to hold off his orgasm.

"Oh God. Ian! I'm...I'm coming."

His hand flew over his cock while his other fondled his balls. He felt his cum boiling inside, racing to his cock, and just as she screamed through the line, he roared, jettisoning his release. He kept stroking until the last spurt fled his body, and then he slumped back onto the bed, dragging in air like he'd just run a mile.

"Now I'm not a phone sex virgin anymore either," he said.

She laughed a throaty, exhausted sound, making his balls quiver in anticipation again because he was the reason she was worn out. How could his cock begin to stir so quickly after that amazing orgasm? He shook his head while he grabbed his t-shirt to clean himself up.

At least she did laugh. He was worried she'd immediately regret this as soon as they'd finished, but so far, it seemed she was okay with it. That was good because he knew he wouldn't stop now. No way was he finished with her. He realized getting involved with her on any level wasn't a good idea, but he'd been attracted to her for a long time, and he wanted to possess her. It wasn't truly possible in their everyday lives, so he'd have to settle for a digital possession, looking at this as another experience that'd be fun to explore. And explore it, he would.

"Get some sleep, Cassie. I'll talk to you tomorrow."

"Is that an order?" He could hear the smile in her voice, and he chuckled at her playfulness.

"Yeah, baby. It is. You need your rest because I intend to have my way with you again tomorrow."

"Hmm. I can't wait."

Neither could he.

———

CASSIE GOT out of the shower the next morning and put on a short skirt and low-cut top over her black lingerie. She also sprayed on some perfume, though she didn't know why she bothered with it. It wasn't as if Ian would be able to smell her. She left her hair down and applied makeup with tones that accentuated her green eyes. Throwing on a few accessories and her pumps, she was ready.

Ian had told her to get some sleep, and boy, did she ever. Her orgasm was one for the record books, going on and on. The Energizer Bunny had nothing on her.

When she thought back over their conversation, it was hard for her to pinpoint when they both left the house of uncomfortable and barreled right into Hornyville, but she was glad they did. It wasn't as if he was her boss, or she was his. They were colleagues, each at the same level as the other, but the company did have a policy on interoffice romance. They'd both have to be careful going forward.

Then she laughed. It wasn't as if either of them had touched the other. A technicality, but one easily argued if the need arose. The fact that he hadn't even laid a hand on her and he was still able to give her the best orgasm of her life spoke volumes. Volumes!

When she showed up at her office, humming to herself and sipping her coffee, she should have known Sasha's internal radar would home in on her. Sasha's head popped up out of her cubicle like a gopher on a golf course, intent on doing the most damage possible. She burrowed her way through the rows, heading straight for Cassie. At least Sasha's damage was of the non-physical kind.

"Well, well, well, if it ain't Miss Tucker. I'm glad to see you're feeling better today."

Oh right. She *did* call in sick yesterday. It'd probably seem a little suspicious if she didn't tone down her chipper attitude. "Yes, I am doing better today. Thanks." She walked to her cubicle with Sasha in tow.

"And looking better. If that skirt were any shorter, you'd be able to see your cooter-cue."

"Gawd, Sasha Ann." Cassie slapped Sasha's arm as she wagged her eyebrows.

"So what happened?" she whispered.

Cassie tried to sigh, but her smile negated any frustration she tried to show. She knew she wouldn't be able to keep this from Sasha, so she told her the details, minus the Dom/sub stuff, while they both drank their java. Sasha maintained her cool because of where they were. Only her eyes getting bigger showed any signs of emotion. When Richard walked up, they both straightened, and Cassie pulled up some work to cover their private conversation.

"Glad to see you back today, Tucker."

"Yeah, must've been allergies." She shrugged as she toggled screens, and Sasha made her escape.

"How's it coming with Cope?"

"Er, Ian is really good. We got all the needed changes documented and submitted to the development team. Should be ready tomorrow for us to test."

"Good, good. Keep me posted," he said as he walked off.

An IM from Sasha popped up on Cassie's laptop.

So you've had sex with the man twice now without him actually penetrating you. Can't say that's ever happened to me.

Cassie chuckled at Sasha's comment. What could she say? It was true.

Yeah. And since he lives in another state, I

have a feeling that's the only way we'll ever have sex.

She didn't know why the thought of that suddenly bothered her. Okay, so she did know why. Ian was hot, but Cassie was finding herself attracted to him in more ways than just his looks. That didn't bode well for her unless she wanted a long-distance relationship.

Let's grab drinks after work. You need to show off that knockout bod of yours.

Cassie laughed. *Sure, I'm game.*

Cassie's email dinged, forcing her to check it since she was actually at work and needed to focus on her job. It was a meeting notification from Mac for a status update. In ten minutes. Crap!

Gotta go. Have a meeting in ten with Mac.

All righty. Good luck.

Cassie called the IT guy to set up the video conference, and then she ran to the restroom. Normally she'd make a pit stop before a meeting for the sole purpose of relieving herself, but she had an ulterior motive now. Ian was also listed as an attendee on the meeting notice, so she wanted to make sure she looked killer. Once she freshened up, she grabbed her notebook and laptop and headed to the conference room. The video conference was up when she walked in.

"Good morning, Tucker," Mac said.

"Cope stepped out for a second." Cassie took a seat and set up her laptop, glancing at the screen to see that Ian was already set up. Then he walked in. "Here he is now."

Her gaze shot to him when he came into view. Lord have mercy, he was sexy. Tan slacks, fitted shirt, coral tie. His disheveled hair looked as unruly as ever, like he just finished taking a roll in the hay. Yum.

"Good morning, Cassie," Ian said as he sat at his computer. He was the cool professional, acting as if nothing had happened between them. She felt the tension leave her shoulders in relief. She didn't anticipate him waltzing in and ordering her to strip, but she really didn't know what to expect.

"Morning, Ian." She adjusted in her seat, playing with her necklace while she stole covert glances at him.

"I just wanted to touch base with the two of you to find out where you are on this project," Mac stated before sipping what had to have been coffee.

"Shouldn't Richard be in here?" Cassie asked. Ian looked down, and Mac cleared his throat.

"No need, Tucker. I'll give him an update later."

She didn't like the sound of this. Office politics could get ugly and in no way was she going to allow Mac to stir up trouble when there was none, especially if that trouble involved her. He could weasel his way into drama in another office. She leveled her gaze on him, gathering her courage to confront him. "Richard is my boss, Mac. Not you. I respect that you called this meeting, but as my boss, Richard should have at least been notified, giving him the choice to attend or not."

Mac's face turned beet red, and he pointed an accusing finger in her direction. Cassie swallowed, bracing herself for his ire. The last thing she wanted was to be taken to task by Ian's boss with him watching. "You listen to me, Tucker. I—"

Ian grabbed Mac's arm. "She's right, Mac. Richard is her boss, and she has to answer to him. It's professional courtesy to notify him of any meetings." He looked in Cassie's direction. "I apologize for the oversight. We'll make sure he's notified in the future."

Cassie wasn't taking the chance. While Ian was coming to her defense, which pleased her greatly, she opened her IM and sent Richard a message letting him know what was going on. If he came barreling through the conference room door, then so be it. She wouldn't mind watching Mac take the brunt of his irritation. Because regardless of what Ian said, Cassie got the feeling Richard not being notified wasn't just an oversight. It was deliberate on Mac's part. He was the one who scheduled this meeting. He should've notified her boss.

"Thank you, but I just informed him that I got called into a meeting. It may not be an issue since I gave him a status update this morning." She tried to make light of the problem Mac created for Ian's benefit. She didn't want to cause any trouble for him.

"Well, if we're through whining about Richard, can we please get on with this?" Mac grumbled as he shifted in his seat.

Ian and Cassie both acquiesced and took turns bringing Mac up to speed. She thought Mac should've been more pleased with their progress. At least he didn't bitch about where they were on this project, but he wasn't exactly singing their praises either. When they finished, they all stood while shutting down their laptops. Although it was very subtle, Cassie heard Ian's sudden intake of breath. She glanced up and saw his eyes smoldering.

"Mac, I have a few more things to discuss with Cassie about the test plan. I'll kill the meeting when we're finished."

Mac mumbled and waved a dismissive hand in Ian's direction. Then he picked up his laptop and left the room. Ian just stood there, staring at her, not saying anything. Without taking his eyes off her, he reached over and picked up the remote for the video conference system. His eyes were predatory, stalking her every breath.

"W-What are you doing?"

"Zooming in. Turn around," he ordered softly.

Trembling at his authoritative sound, she obeyed, moving away from her chair and turning slowly.

"Jesus, Cass, you need to be spanked for coming to work dressed like that." He groaned, and she looked over her shoulder at him. "Bend over."

She hesitated. She was at work, in the conference room...with the door unlocked. Richard never responded to her IM, so theoretically, he could come barging in at any second, catching her.

And that made it even hotter.

"Don't make me tell you again," he warned gently.

Cassie slowly bent over, touching her toes.

"God, baby, I can almost see your ass cheeks. Lift you skirt. Show me that sweet little ass of yours."

Cassie groaned as she slid her hand around and gathered her skirt at the side, drawing it up. When she'd put on the black lingerie this morning, she'd hoped Ian would get to see it. Now he was about to. Just the thought of him looking at the scrap of black lace that barely covered her made her pussy wet.

"Fuck, Cassie," he breathed. "Stand up

and look at me."

She dropped her skirt and turned around, facing him, relieved to be out of her compromising position, yet regretting that her little teasing show seemed to be over.

"I want you on Skype tonight. Right after work."

"Can't. Going out with Sasha for drinks," she said casually as she shrugged a shoulder, hiding her smile.

"Drinks? With Sasha? Wearing that?"

"Yes. Yes. Yes." She did smile then and started gathering her things.

"You're going to get hit on by every drunk motherfucker in that bar." He didn't sound mad, but he did sound a little possessive. She rather liked that.

"Oh, I know."

"Don't let another man touch what's mine, Cassie."

"Yours? How do you figure?"

He growled. "You like being sassy don't you?"

She laughed. "Sassy Cassie. Now there's a blast from the past. My best friend in high school used to call me that."

He sighed, clearly not really finding the amusement. "I'm serious, baby."

He sounded serious, too. And not in an ordering-her-around kind of way. He sounded worried. She didn't even want to begin to process the meaning of that.

"Look, I have to go before someone walks in."

"Fine. Be on Skype at ten."

"What if I'm not back by then?"

"You will be." Then he disconnected the meeting.

CHAPTER SIX

"There she is!" Sasha yelled when Cassie walked into the bar. Luckily, the place was loud enough that not many people turned around to see who she was yelling at.

"I'll have a dirty martini," Cassie said to the bartender as she hopped onto the stool next to her friend. "Make that a strong one, darlin'."

"You got it, babe." He winked at her as he set about making her drink.

"Where were you all afternoon, Sasha? I looked everywhere for you."

She wrinkled her nose. "You didn't check the server room. I've been doing backup since Marty's out of town."

The bartender placed her drink in front of her and threw her a crooked smile before walking away. She took a sip and moaned. Damn, but that was a strong drink.

"Holy hell, Chip was totally checking you out," Sasha all but squealed.

"What?" Cassie looked around, holding her drink to her lips. "Who?" She turned back to Sasha. "Where?"

"The bartender."

Cassie shrugged. The guy was definitely a looker, but she knew how this game was played. "He's in it for the tips. Don't let him sucker you." She chuckled.

"Oh no, I've been here a few different times, and he's always all business. Sure, he'll yap it up if he has time, but he's usually too busy to flirt."

"He was not flirting with me," Cassie mumbled into her delicious drink.

"Whateva." Sasha ran her hand through her short locks, scrunching her hair. "So why were you looking for me earlier?"

"Oh. Different reasons." Cassie took a big gulp and set her drink down, leaning toward Sasha. "Boring stuff first. You know that meeting I had earlier? Well, Dick Weiner wasn't invited to come play."

"Hmm. So the Mac Daddy skirted protocol. What's up with that?" Sasha downed the rest of her frozen drink and waved her empty glass at Chip.

"Don't know. But it's a little suspicious, don't you think? To be honest, there aren't very many changes that need to be made to that application. Ian's office could've handled it without our involvement at all."

Chip refreshed Sasha's frozen delight, giving her a brief smile before turning his attention to Cassie. "You doin' okay, babe?"

Cassie nodded, sipping greedily at her martini. He winked at her again as he walked away.

"Told you," Sasha murmured as she took a drink. Cassie rolled her eyes and waved her hand dismissively at Sasha. It didn't matter what Chip thought of her. Ian's directive for Cassie not to let any man touch her played on a seductive loop in her head. Sasha set her drink down and looked at Cassie. "I don't know what to think about that. It does seem odd. Maybe Mac likes ruling the roost."

"I just have a weird feeling about this."

"Well, not to sound like a total bitch, but I didn't skip Farmville to come out and have drinks and talk about work," Sasha said with a laugh as she picked her drink back up. "I hope the other reason you were searching me out earlier today is juicer than office shenanigans."

Cassie took a big gulp of her drink, finishing it, finding the courage to bring up the next topic. Then she pulled out the olives and started eating them, letting the tart juice burst in her mouth. Within seconds, Chip had another martini sitting in front of her. She glanced up at him as he walked away, still watching her as he left. He winked when she made eye contact, then filled another customer's drink order.

"Okay. This conversation stays between us. If you so much as breathe another word of this to anybody, Sasha, I'll tell Paul from accounting that you have the biggest crush on him."

"Eww. Gross. I'd rather eat dog shit. And I mean the white, putrefied shit that no one likes to clean up."

Cassie threw her head back and laughed. Sasha was a bit of a drama queen, but she was funny as hell. She enjoyed hanging out with her every chance she got.

Cassie's laughter drew Chip's attention. He walked to their end of the bar, tossing a towel over his shoulder. "You ladies havin' a good time?" Though the question was posed to both, he was staring right at Cassie.

"Yeah, thanks," Cassie said.

Luckily, a customer asked for a mixed drink, so he walked away, keeping him from getting into a deeper conversation.

"I'm surprised you don't reek of urine," Sasha said to Cassie. "Because Chip is pissing all over you, marking you as his."

Cassie choked on her drink and gawked at Sasha. "Are you out of your mind? He's just being nice."

"Oh please, girl. I admit, it's been a while since I've had a man go all territorial on me, but I know when a guy is staking a claim. And that one over there is about to grab you by the hair and drag you back to his cave."

"He should get in line," Cassie mumbled as she swallowed an olive.

Sasha's eyes got really big, and she slammed her drink down. "Oh my God. Is Ian staking a claim?"

"Oh yeah. He's definitely doing his share of pissing."

Sasha laughed, clapping her hands. "That's awesome, girl! Of course I hate your guts."

Cassie giggled. "I know, right? I'm a little overwhelmed, which is what I need to talk to you about."

Sasha nodded seriously as she picked up her glass and took a sip. "Spill. And I'll take it to the grave."

Cassie took a deep breath. "Have you ever been with a dominant guy?"

Sasha frowned. "You mean like whips and chains and shit? Why would any woman since the feminist movement be into that?" She shrugged as she brought her drink up to her mouth and then hesitated. Her gaze shot to Cassie's. "Good Lord! Ian's a Dom?"

"Hush! I don't want everybody knowing my business. But no, he's not really a Dom. He's just *dominant*."

"Er, what's the difference?"

Cassie groaned. This conversation wasn't

going how she wanted it to. "He's sexually assertive. But not into the full lifestyle. I've been with a Dom before and really liked it, but it wasn't a life calling for me either."

"Hold up. You were a sub?" Sasha stared at Cassie with an unfathomable expression. It could've been worse. She could've stared at her in disgust, but her eyes twinkled with something akin to interest and maybe a little amusement. "When did this happen? And why am I just now finding out?"

"A few years ago. I met this guy. I had an itch. He scratched it. End of story."

"That's a big ol' pile of bullshit right there. I want deets!"

"Damn, girl. What do you want me to say?"

"Just start talking. I'll let you know when it's enough, which, by the way, won't be until you get to the part where you let a guy top you."

Cassie shook her head but smiled. "He was a stockbroker I met through my financial advisor. He asked me out, and on our first date, he told me what he was into. Said it was his way of life, not some fantasy. He didn't pressure me or anything. Just laid it all out there. We went out a couple of times after that, and when I wanted to dip my toes into the submissive pool, he was eager to guide me. Guide me?" She chuckled. "More like throw me into the deep end. It was hot as hell, but like I said, it wasn't for me. He wanted a full sub, someone to take care of and cherish. I didn't want someone feeding me and giving me baths all the time. Every now and then? Yeah, that'd be really sweet. But every damn day? I'd be pulling my hair out before he'd get a chance to brush it for me."

"I'm sorry, but feminist alarms are sounding off in my head. I couldn't let a man control me like that. I'm not a weak person."

Cassie sighed. "That's just it, Sasha. I think it takes an incredibly strong woman to submit. It takes a great deal of power to trust a man strong enough to give him that kind of control. The right man understands the gift that that is."

"And the wrong man can abuse the power given to him. Some guys take too much anyway." Sasha frowned. Something dark flashed across her gaze, but it disappeared just as quickly. "I see what you're saying, though. I know it's very empowering when a guy loses himself during sex. I guess I can see the appeal for some, but no way is a guy going to tell me what to do. In or out of the sack." She laughed.

Cassie sucked on another olive. "I need to go. I'm supposed to be online at ten."

"Mmm. You gonna get your kink on?" Sasha smirked.

"You know it. Regardless of the fact Ian is

in another state and I'll probably never have real sex with him, that man knows how to work it. And I'm going to love every minute of it."

"Atta girl!" Sasha laughed as she downed the last of her fruity concoction. "At least you're getting some. The last action I saw was six months ago. Woo hoo!" She pumped her fist in the air to drive home her sarcastic comment, which made Cassie snort, spewing her drink across the bar.

"Girl, you're cracking my stuff up! I know you just didn't rock the fist pump right here in the middle of this bar." She laughed.

"Hell, it's the only thing I get to rock nowadays. Let me have some fun." Something dark flashed across Sasha eyes before she straightened and pouted playfully as she motioned for Chip to close out their tabs.

He walked over with their receipts. They took them, and he never took his eyes off Cassie. She looked down and saw a zero balance.

"Tonight's on me," Chip said with a smile.

"Thanks," they both said in unison.

Chip flashed his eyes at Sasha and smiled before looking back at Cassie and leaning closer to her. "I'd also like Friday night to be on me too. Say dinner and a movie?"

Cassie suppressed a gasp, but she saw Sasha grinning from ear to ear and couldn't help the heat that flushed her face. Cassie wasn't used to such a blatant come-on, and she had absolutely no idea how to handle this. If it wasn't for Ian, she'd accept. Chip was a good-looking guy. Tall, muscular but not bulky, light-blue eyes and a goatee. Definitely drool worthy.

But there *was* Ian. And Cassie didn't want to do anything to mess up what was happening between the two of them. But not only that, she just didn't want another man. Oh boy, she didn't want to think about what that meant.

"Look," Cassie sighed. "I'm totally flattered—"

"Uh-oh," he mumbled. "If you tell me I'm a really great guy to soften this blow, I think it just might kill me." He laughed, and damn was that a sexy sound.

Cassie chuckled. "You *are* a really great guy."

"Ouch." He clasped his heart and stumbled back a few steps theatrically, then stepped up to her again, leaning his elbows on the bar, coming closer to her. "He's a lucky man. Whoever he is."

"He is." And whoever snagged Chip would be one lucky gal.

He leaned back and crossed his arms over his chest, all business now. "You girls okay to drive home?"

"We're good," Sasha said and grabbed

Cassie's arm to drag her away from the bar. "Told ya he was pissing all over you," she murmured as they walked out the bar and into the parking lot. But Cassie only wanted one man staking a claim. "Yeah, you're good and all that shit. I'll catch you later."

Sasha gave her a sassy little wave as she walked to her car, and Cassie shook her head as she got into her own vehicle.

What seemed like forever but was really only about ten minutes later, she pulled into her driveway, walked into her house and tossed her purse on the table. It was almost ten, so she had just enough time to pee and brush her teeth. Why she bothered with the latter, she didn't know. It wasn't as if she'd be kissing Ian.

She felt a pang of sadness at that thought. What would kissing him be like? She wondered if his kiss would be forceful or tender and eventually settled on something in between. His kiss would be self-confident and controlled by him, but he'd take care in exploring every inch of her mouth. He'd nip at her lips while his hand would be wrapped protectively around her nape. The other hand would be buried in her hair, guiding her where he wanted her. He'd kiss her so passionately she'd have to break away to gasp for breath, but he'd just pepper kisses along her jaw and neck, refusing to take his lips off her body while she tried to remember to inhale.

Yeah, kissing him would be spectacular, but she'd only ever get to fantasize. No matter how much she'd love his mouth on hers, it just wasn't going to happen.

Cassie booted up her laptop and logged on to Skype. As soon as she was online, she got a video call from Ian. He was already on and waiting for her.

"Hi," she said when he came into view. Holy cow, he was hot! He had on a muscle shirt and pajama pants. He was sitting on the chair with one foot on the seat and his arm hanging over the knee that was up beside his head. And he was barefoot. God, even his foot was sexy.

"Hey. When did you get in?" He took a swig from the beer he'd been dangling over his knee.

"Just got here."

He nodded. "You wanna get something to drink? I'd offer you something, but..." He motioned toward the screen, emphasizing his inability to actually play host.

She chuckled. "Yeah, give me a sec." Cassie got up, walked into her kitchen and plucked a bottle of wine off the shelf, grabbing a glass and corkscrew on her way back to her bedroom.

"So did you have fun tonight?" Ian asked as Cassie sat down and opened her wine.

"Yeah. Hung out with Sasha." She flashed her eyes up from the task at hand to look in his direction. "Got hit on by the bartender."

He made a noncommittal sound as he drank from his bottle. He tried to play it cool, but his eyes betrayed his nonchalant behavior. He didn't like the idea of another man hitting on her. She hid her smile.

"What did you do tonight?"

"Talked to my bother. Watched the game." He shrugged. "You know, bartenders only flirt for the tips."

She did smile then. "That's what I told Sasha, but she didn't believe me. Of course when he paid for our drinks and asked me out, I realized it wasn't dollar signs he was after when he laid on the charm."

His eyes narrowed, and he stopped his beer in the middle of its progression to his mouth. "He asked you out?" Incredulity filled his voice.

"I'm not sure if I should be offended by that question or not. I do get asked out from time to time, Ian." She smirked.

"And what did you say?" he asked right away, not commenting on her remark.

"I turned him down."

He seemed slightly mollified. "Why?" He leaned back into his seat and finally took that drink he initiated before she dropped the news of her dinner offer on him.

What could she tell him? If she said she didn't want to see other people, he might think she was obsessed with him. It wasn't as if they were in a relationship. Heck, they hadn't even gone out on a date themselves. Wasn't she just thinking about the fact that they'd never even get to kiss for real?

"I just didn't want to." She poured her wine and took a drink immediately to cover her nerves.

"Stand up."

Cassie's gaze shot to him, and he stared at her with an unreadable expression. Setting her glass down, she slowly stood.

He reached over and turned on an MP3 player. The slow, seductive song drifted through the speaker as if she'd turned it on in her bedroom. "Strip."

She balked. It was obvious he didn't just want her to take her clothes off. He wanted her to dance for him, and this went a little beyond her comfort level. She wasn't some twenty-two-year-old stripper. She was already a little nervous about him seeing her fully naked, and rightly so, but the thought of not only undressing but parading around like she had a body to flaunt caused paranoia to flood her body.

"Cassie, I'll never ask anything of you that you can't do. You have a beautiful body, and I want you to show me how sexy *you* think you are. Now strip for me, baby. Show me what's mine."

What is his. He viewed her as his. The

butterflies in her stomach multiplied. She was nervous, no doubt about that, but she also felt a sense of pride, knowing Ian thought she was beautiful and wanted her for himself. Even if he was just creating an aura of possession for play, it was still erotic and definitely fed her ego, making her want to prove him right about how sexy she could be.

Cassie reached up, traced her finger along her neck as her head fell back, gliding her finger to her exposed cleavage. She swayed her hips in time with the sensual music, then turned, giving him her back. She brought her hands up to her hair, gathering it up on her head as she shimmied down and back up, swaying seductively to the music. She heard Ian's soft curse and felt a spike of adrenaline, knowing he was already affected by her performance and she hadn't taken off a lick of clothing yet. She reached for the hem of her shirt and slid it up her sides, almost to her breasts. Then she pulled it back down teasingly.

Ian groaned.

Cassie treated her skirt the same way, pulling it up almost to her buttocks and dropping it before he got a chance to see the goods. She grabbed the hem of her shirt again, but this time, she pulled it off and turned to face him.

He licked his lips as she gathered her hair again and shimmied down before rocking her hips on the way back up. She teased him by pulling one of her bra straps off her shoulder but left it there. Reaching for her skirt, she eased it up her thighs as she widened her stance. She pulled it all the way up to her waist and squatted as she cupped her sex with one hand and kneaded her breast with the other.

Ian's breathing got louder, but Cassie didn't look at him. She had her eyes shut, lost in the moment.

She clutched the top of her skirt and unfastened it, letting it fall to the floor. Now she danced before him in her black lace bra and panties. She reached behind and unclasped her bra, turning around before it fell to the floor. She swayed her hips, shaking her thong-covered ass for his viewing pleasure. Then she dipped her head and flung her hair as she turned back toward him, hands covering her breasts.

"Damn, baby," he breathed.

She caught him moving out of the corner of her eye. He'd taken off his shirt and was now unzipping his pants. Eyes locked on her. She turned back around, widening her stance again, and bent over at the waist. She ran her finger along the seam of her ass before caressing both cheeks.

"That's it, baby. Show me that pretty little ass of yours."

She grabbed the tiny straps and yanked

her panties down, stepping out of them. Still bending over, she spread her cheeks apart, giving him a view of the promise land.

He groaned and there was more rustling on his end. Cassie righted herself and turned slowly, rubbing her hands along her hips as she faced him completely nude.

He was naked now too, stroking his cock as he watched her.

"God, Cassie. You're so fucking beautiful."

She stalked toward him. "I'm glad you like."

"I love. Get on the bed, closer to your computer."

She crawled on the bed with her backside facing him, but she looked over her shoulder to watch him as she got into position.

"Sit and spread your legs." Cassie turned around and sat, opening up for him. "That's it, baby. Move the camera closer so I can see that sweet pussy."

Cassie's body was on fire. The little dance she did got her all wet and ready for him, and now it wouldn't take much for her to come. She did his bidding, leaning back and stretching herself open with her fingers, wanting to rub her clit but waiting for his command.

"Fuck! You're already drenched, baby.

You know what I'd do if I were there right now?" he asked as he stroked his cock slowly.

"What?" she asked breathlessly. She couldn't wait to hear what he'd do.

"I'd bury my face between your legs, shove my tongue in that hot pussy and drink the honey from your body as you fed it to me."

Cassie moaned and her fingers twitched to rub the folds of her pussy, push inside, play with her clit, anything. She just wanted to touch herself.

"Lick your taut nipple for me, baby. Show me you can do it."

Cassie grabbed her breast and pushed it up as her tongue descended. It swiped over the nipple and she moaned at the flavor. "Mmm. Tastes so good."

He hissed in a breath. "Shit, Cass, I'm not going to be able to last long like this. Touch yourself. Make yourself come for me."

Her hand trailed back down her body and she jerked as soon as her finger made contact with her pulsing clit.

"God, Ian. I wish it were you touching me."

"Yeah, baby. I'd tease that clit until you were ready to scream my name."

She threw her head back and moaned as she rubbed it harder and pushed a finger into her pussy. When she heard him groan, she looked at him, seeing him watching her. "You have such a big cock. Damn, but I wish it were you inside me right now."

His eyes narrowed as he stroked faster. "You think you could take all of me?" His arrogant question didn't really need answering. Cassie could tell that if Ian were pushing inside her, he'd make sure she took all he had to offer. Her pussy spasmed with the onset of her orgasm. She was almost there.

"I'd take it all in one hard thrust. Make you feel my pussy squeeze around you as I come."

"Baby, I'd throw you on the bed and shove my dick so hard inside you that you'd try to come off the bed but couldn't because I'd be pinning you down. You'd feel me everywhere. Know who owned you."

She gasped at his possessive tone and rubbed her clit faster.

He groaned and quickened his strokes. "Ahhh, yes, baby. Are you going to come for me?" His voice was hoarse.

She whimpered, couldn't speak. Her vision became blurry, but she forced herself to keep her eyes open. She wanted to watch him come apart. The burning in her belly intensified, and her hips lifted off the bed. She fucked herself faster as her climax built.

"Ian!" she yelled, her world shattering around her. She barely heard his guttural growl breaking through her haze of euphoria. She opened her eyes to see Ian's chest glistening with the sweat he produced through his efforts to prolong his release. His procrastination was no longer viable. The muscles in his neck were corded as he strained through his orgasm.

He wasn't easy with his body. His hand tormented the pulsing erection as he shot stream after stream of cum onto his belly. He groaned as he brought himself down and made eye contact with Cassie once again.

The emotion she saw in his gaze staggered her. If she wasn't so sure he'd be smart about this and not fall in love with her when there wasn't a chance for them, she'd swear his feelings mirrored her own.

And she suddenly realized she wasn't smart about this.

CHAPTER SEVEN

By Friday the application was ready, allowing Ian and Cassie an opportunity to test it thoroughly and tweak it as needed. Cassie was full of wonderful ideas and very knowledgeable about her job and the industry as a whole. Ian was finding himself more and more impressed with her abilities the more time he spent with her.

He was also finding himself unable to get her off his mind when he wasn't spending time with her. He thought about her nonstop to the point that during the day, he'd send her text messages with naughty little innuendos... and blatant come-ons. Then at night, they'd spend hours masturbating for the other's viewing pleasure. And still he was unable to assuage his growing need for her. It was the hottest relationship he'd ever had, yet he wasn't truly with her. Just the thought of not really being with her had his heart howling in protest, but he couldn't bring himself to examine what that meant.

Prior to Aaron giving him a taste of the Dom/sub life, Ian had an inkling that his dominant desire smoldered beneath the surface. The experience that Aaron had provided just emphasized that knowledge, but Ian had never felt the surge of possessiveness with another woman before Cassie. Now he couldn't bank the demand his body was trying to make on him to claim her in every way possible. He knew he was becoming more and more demanding of her, which she seemed to relish. And he fed off that. Whenever she'd send him a text, call him or talk to him online, his insides would scream *Mine!* It took an exorbitant amount of strength to keep that declaration from being verbalized. Though at the height of his passion, it slipped one way or another, but he'd hoped Cassie chalked it up to him being caught in the moment.

Or did he?

Hell, he didn't know. He didn't want to explore what that meant, either, because he knew all of it was related to his feelings. Feelings he had no right to embrace.

Ignorance was bliss. A fucking painful bliss.

He didn't know what to do about this mess with Mac. He had an obligation to do his job, but he was discovering his work wasn't his sole responsibility. The only way he felt he was able to work on the consolidation plan for the closure of Cassie's office was if he stayed unemotional and looked at it as just another duty. Yeah, he knew it was a shitty way to approach it, but he had no choice. And so whenever Ian had spoken to Cassie, he always made sure he'd asked causal questions about her job, coworkers, assignments and general office dynamics. He'd had enough information to effectively reassign current projects to offices with minimal impact to the other locations.

Ian spent the afternoon finalizing this dreaded part of Mac's orders. He hated being put in this position, so the sooner he could finish it, the better he'd feel.

And the sooner Cassie would lose her job. *Where's your protectiveness of her now?* he thought wryly.

When he finished, Ian emailed the documentation to Mac and strolled into his office. He didn't want to wait until Monday to talk to Mac about this. Ian wanted it over now. He rounded the hallway and pounded on his boss's office door.

"Come in," Mac called.

Ian walked in and sat in front of Mac's desk. "I just sent you the completed consolidation plan."

"Good, good," he said distractedly as he fumbled with some forms on his messy desk.

Then he looked up at Ian. "What about the software modification?"

"Almost finished. We tested and submitted a few changes. It should be ready Monday."

Mac sat forward. "Excellent. I have a meeting with the executive staff on Tuesday. I'll present everything then. In the meantime, I'll look over your material and let you know if I have any questions."

Mac turned back to his computer, effectively dismissing Ian. He suppressed a growl as he stood and left.

Damn, but he felt two feet tall. He wasn't used to feeling worthless, and when he normally had a bad day, he'd go home and have a beer. But the only thing appealing to him was Cassie. He still had over two hours before time to leave the office, but Cassie would be leaving in about thirty minutes. He could just leave early. He was finished with everything he had pending. But he couldn't even wait the thirty minutes for her to get off and then the other amount of time it'd take for her to get home.

He'd last spoken to her just this morning, but it'd been too long since his last contact. He was quickly becoming an addict, and Cassie was his prized fix that he'd go to any length and pay any price to have.

———

HEY, baby.

Leaning back in her chair at her desk, Cassie reread the text Ian had just sent her. Normally, he was bold in his correspondence with her, but his simple message almost seemed desperate. She wasn't sure how to respond at first and then decided to keep it simple.

Hey, yourself.

Several minutes went by without a response, so Cassie started to wonder if he was even going to reply. A few minutes later, her phone went off, acknowledging an incoming text. She smiled. There he was.

Send me a picture of your breasts. I need to see them.

She chuckled as she pushed the phone back enough to snap a shot of her clothed breasts and sent it to him. She did show a little cleavage, but she knew that wasn't all Ian wanted to see. If he wanted to see more, he'd have to tell her. She liked it when he told her exactly what he wanted. It was freeing in a way not having to guess. After an agonizing minute, she got another message from him.

Nice. Now go to the bathroom, unbutton your shirt, pull your breasts out over your bra and send me a photo of that.

Cassie followed his orders, going into the last stall to do his bidding. Just as she was about to take the picture, she got a devious little idea. Rather than taking a picture of her exposed breasts, she'd take one of her exposed belly up to the bottom of her bra. No boob shot. She quickly snapped the image and sent it to him. He immediately responded.

Well, Sassy Cassie, if I could, I'd spank that little ass for your insolence. She chuckled at the use of her old nickname, the sound echoing against the tile.

I don't know what you're talking about. She threw on a smiley face at the end of her message.

Now, baby. You know exactly what you did by teasing me with the photo of your very sexy tummy. Now send me one of those beautiful breasts.

She'd followed his order, sending the picture. Her phone rang immediately afterward.

"Now that's what I call a sexy woman," Ian's voice poured over the line as soon as Cassie answered.

"I'm glad you think so."

"I know so," he sighed, and she frowned at his sad tone as she started buttoning her shirt back up.

"Something wrong?"

He hesitated, and she paused in adjusting her shirt, waiting to hear what he had to say. "Bad day."

She wasn't sure what he meant by that. The project they were working on was priority and currently with the development team making the final changes. But she also knew Ian was responsible for other projects.

"You want talk about it?"

"No," he said quickly.

He was definitely on edge for whatever reason, and she didn't like that. She wanted him at ease, and she would like nothing more than to be the reason for the turnaround in his mood. While she thought about her wishes to please him, an idea formed in her head. "You free tonight?"

He chuckled, and she smiled at the sexy sound. "I'm always free for you."

Her heart fluttered while the blood raced to her face, but she tamped down her silly nerves. "Good. Meet me online at seven."

She hung up the phone, not giving him a chance to respond. She had work to do and not a lot of time to do it. She ran out of the bathroom and back to her desk. She closed up shop for the weekend, shutting down her laptop and grabbing her purse, then headed straight for Sasha's desk.

"Hey, I need your help. I'm calling in all my girlfriend favors."

Sasha leaned back in her chair with a saucy grin. "I gotta hear this."

"Grab your purse, and I'll explain on the way."

She followed Cassie to the parking lot and jumped into the passenger seat. "Where are we going?"

"Er, a toy shop," Cassie said as she pulled out of her parking space.

Sasha cackled and bounced in her seat like a kid on Christmas morning. "You shouldn't need a battery-operated boyfriend. You've got a living, breathing one."

Cassie slanted her eyes at Sasha. "Ian's not my boyfriend, but I want to surprise him. The nature of our relation—er, arrangement makes it impossible to be with him physically, so I have to improvise."

"Oh, I like the sound of this." Sasha rubbed her hands together as she wagged her eyebrows.

"You say that now. Wait until I call in the favors."

Sasha narrowed her gaze on Cassie. "What's that mean? Having me go with you to the toy store to hold your hand while you buy a rubber dong isn't the favor?" She tried to be serious, but she smirked anyway.

"Nope. I said I was calling in *all* the favors." A few minutes later Cassie pulled up to their destination. "C'mon."

The girls got out, walked into the store and stared at all the fun paraphernalia. Cassie soon realized she was way out of her element. When she played with her stockbroker friend, he utilized many devices, so she had a frame of reference. But now that she was here, she felt a little intimidated. After taking a fortifying breath, she trudged over to the massive dildo selection. She didn't have time to hide behind humility.

"Whoa, look at this hawse!" Sasha grabbed the giant rubber phallus on display, slinging it around.

"Good grief!" Cassie said, shaking her head. "I can't take you anywhere."

Sasha chuckled, putting it back down. "What kinda dildo do you want to get?"

Cassie shrugged, looking round. "I don't know. I guess something like this might work." She picked up the one attached to a strap-on harness.

Sasha eyed her critically. "Are you planning on fucking somebody with that? I thought you wanted one to use on yourself."

Cassie frowned. "Oh, I do." She shrugged, struggling for the right way to explain what she wanted. "I, er, I figured it'd make things easier if I could find one that allows me to strap it on somehow to keep it inserted."

"Ah, okay." Sasha looked down the row and stopped, grabbing a box. "Bluetooth?"

"Huh?" Cassie walked over to her.

"This one has Bluetooth capabilities." She pursed her lips while she read the instructions. "Looks like it can be controlled remotely with the right access codes."

"Oh my God, next thing you know, there'll be an app for these suckers for every smartphone on the market." Cassie chuckled but then seriously thought about it. "Hey, let me see it," she said as she snatched it out of Sasha's hand.

"Damn, girl, you'd have to take out a second mortgage to buy this one."

"Yeah, but if Ian could control it, then it'd be a small price to pay."

Recognition lit Sasha's eyes. "You're one freaky bitch." She laughed. "He's gonna have a heart attack when he realizes he gets to have more control over your pleasure."

"That's the idea."

And it was perfect. Looked like a simple registration and a link for Ian to access would be all that was needed. With one toy out of the way, Cassie set off to find the other things she needed. She grabbed some nipple clamps, red lingerie, handcuffs and scarves. She was running on nervous energy as she paid for her stash, walked to her car and drove back to the office to drop off Sasha.

"I don't mean to burst your bubble or anything, Cass, but you do realize you can't be completely strapped down."

"What do you mean?"

"I mean, you have to have at least one hand free to work your gadgets. But he'll still flip his lid when he sees you."

They pulled up to Sasha's car and Cassie turned toward her. "I plan on being completely strapped down. Now that Ian will be able to control the device, there's no need for me to have a free hand."

Sasha laughed in confusion. "Yeah, but how do you expect to connect to the video call and, more importantly, get free once you've had your boom-boom?"

Cassie smiled innocently at Sasha. "About those favors."

CHAPTER EIGHT

"I can't believe you talked me into this!" Sasha squealed as she pulled a velvet-tipped nipple clamp out of the box.

"Just drink your wine and shut your trap." Cassie giggled as she enjoyed a little bit of liquid courage herself. "We only have about fifteen minutes 'til showtime."

Cassie wrapped the handcuffs around the iron-scrolled headboard and tied the scarves a decent width apart to satisfy both her comfort needs and Ian's viewing pleasure. She'd already changed into the new lingerie and donned a robe to wear while she set up everything.

"You expect me to hang around until you're finished having internet sex with your hottie, so I can help you break free of the bonds of love." She chuckled. "I so don't want to hear you get it on."

"Just go into the living room and play

Farmville. You'll be so wrapped up in that you'll forget what you're doing here."

"Yeah, right. I'll just plant my fake crops while Ian sows his imaginary seed."

"Nothing imaginary about that," Cassie mumbled with a twinkle in her eye. Then she shook her head. "I'll tell Ian to text you when we're finished. But if you don't get anything from him after about two hours, you have my permission to come check on me."

"Just so you know, payback is a *biiootch*." Sasha tossed back the last of her wine as she stood and handed over the nipple clamps.

The lingerie had cutouts at the breasts with a garter belt and stockings. She'd put everything on, sans panties, and had pulled out a pair of matching stilettos. Guys liked it when women wore these dreadfully uncomfortable things, but Cassie had to admit they did look awesome and comfort wouldn't be an issue lying down. She dropped the clamps and picked up her cell phone, sending Ian a text with the link he needed to control her dildo. The message was cryptic enough not to give anything away until she was ready for him to understand.

After that was completed, she latched on the nipple clamps, hissing as pain bloomed. With Sasha turned around, Cassie took off the robe, sat in the middle of her bed and tied her feet to the scarves at the footboard. She maneuvered the dildo in place, securing it and turning it on. Then she leaned back and tied the leash that was affixed to the nipple clamps onto her wrists. If she moved them, it'd tug at the clamps, heightening her arousal. She was very careful not to do anything now to excite herself, because Sasha was still in the room, covertly diverting her gaze, and she didn't want there to be any more awkwardness than what was absolutely necessary. But it was difficult not to get turned-on with the clamps on her sensitive buds and the dildo lodged firmly inside her.

"Okay, I'm ready."

Sasha glanced at her and barked a laugh before quickly stifling it. "Sorry, sorry." She walked over and cuffed Cassie to the headboard. Then walked back over to the laptop, making sure it was positioned for the best access. She draped a shirt over it, covering the attached webcam, so Ian wouldn't be able to see until Cassie was ready for him to. Working around the cloth, Sasha logged on to Cassie's Skype account. "He's already logged on. Damn, he's fast," Sasha said suddenly. "He just sent you a video call. Impatient bastard." She chuckled.

"Accept the call and get behind the computer. Don't pull away the cover until I tell you to."

Sasha nodded. There was no turning back now.

———

IAN WENT to the link Cassie had sent him, but he wasn't sure what it was for. It looked to be controls to something electronic. There wasn't any explanation as to what it was, probably just something around her house, so he wasn't sure what she needed help with. He'd hoped that tonight's "date" would be like the others, but if she needed help with some electronics, then he was happy she'd turned to him. He smiled at that thought. This was a good sign, right? That she'd turned to him like a boyfriend for a helping hand.

He left that window open as he waited for Cassie to connect to Skype. Once she did, he sent her a video call but frowned when she accepted. "Baby, there's something blocking your webcam."

He leaned closer to his screen, trying to make out what was blocking her camera, but he couldn't identify the offending object.

"Oh, I'll get it. Looks like my shirt I changed out of earlier," she said nonchalantly. "Did you get that link I sent you?"

"Got it up now." He popped open a beer as he sat back in his chair, waiting for her to remove the obstruction.

As he took a drink, the material slinked away, revealing the image before him.

The air locked in his lungs and blood

rushed to his groin, creating the fastest, hardest erection of his life. He stared dumbly, frozen for what seemed like hours but what was merely seconds. He then slammed his beer down, leaning closer and staring at the goddess before him, stunned. Completely and utterly stunned.

She watched him, a smile playing at the corners of her succulent lips. "Surprise," she murmured. She could've cast a spell with that one word because all he heard was his own personal siren.

"Fuck me," he whispered incredulously.

"That's the plan."

At that, he groaned. Beer forgotten, he yanked his shirt off his overheated body and immediately unzipped his pants. If he didn't get them off soon, his cock would cause the seams to burst. He stood, stripping out of them, and sighed at the instant relief he felt at his newfound freedom. Now that his skin could breathe, he forced himself to absorb his little vixen's action and find a little control, lest he explode as soon as he touched himself.

He sat back down, gently taking his dick in hand, gritting his teeth against the overwhelming sensation.

"I see you've been a very busy, very *naughty* little girl."

"You seemed like you needed a little pick-me-up."

"Oh, I'm up. I'm so up I could pound

nails with my cock." He took a deep breath as he eased back into a more comfortable position. "Lift your hips, baby. Let me see what you've done."

She raised her pussy and he squeezed his dick when his balls started to tingle. He wouldn't embarrass himself shooting off just yet. But damn it to hell, she was fucking beautiful! He shut his eyes and tried to catch his breath. When he opened them, he focused on her breasts and saw that the nipple clamps she wore were tethered to her wrists. "Lift your arms," he ordered huskily.

She did, whimpering when the action tugged at her sensitive buds.

"That feel good, baby?" He leaned closer, wishing he could step right through the screen and into her bedroom.

She nodded, biting her lip.

"Say it, Cassie. Tell me how it feels."

"It burns. It's shooting sparks straight to my pussy." She moved her arms, pulling at her nipples again. This time she gasped then moaned as she whirled her wrists around.

"That's it, baby. Tease yourself for me." Ian groaned as he stroked his cock and watched the sexy scene unfold before him, too engrossed to think clearly.

"I'd rather you tease me," she said breathlessly.

God, he'd give anything to be touching her himself right now. "Mmm, I know,

Cassie. If I were there, it'd be my teeth biting you instead of those clamps."

She sucked in air as she tugged on them again. Ian liked that she seemed to enjoy the thought of his teeth worrying her nipples. Then she smile seductively. "You can still tease me from there."

Of course he could. He'd been teasing her for days without actually touching her. He just wished he could control her orgasm himself. He knew it was his dominant part barreling to the front of his psyche demanding that control. Knowing she did what he told her when he told her was a fucking turn-on like no other, but being able to bring her to the precipice over and over again without letting her go over would be the icing on the Cassie cake.

She licked her lips. "You got that link up?"

Huh? She wanted to put the brakes on now? "Yeah, baby. It can wait until after we've played. I want to give you my undivided attention." He was already scheming how to get her off because he knew it'd be hard without the use of her hands, but damn, it was sexy as hell seeing her all tied up for him.

"But it's my other surprise for you. Pull it up."

Not knowing what to think, he brought up the small screen. "Okay, so what am I—

Sweet mother of God!" he gasped. "Is this what I think it is?"

Holy shit! No way was this a remote control to something attached to her body. But now that he thought about it, the options for various settings could be just that. He clicked the first one and heard a low hum over the airwaves followed by her moan. His head shot to her just as her hips lifted helplessly off the bed.

"Cassie," he breathed, understanding finally setting in. The link was a control to the vibrator attached to her. For a moment he forgot the fact he'd get his wish fulfilled of controlling her climax, and his heart squeezed in his chest when he realized she went through all this trouble to please him. It couldn't have been easy, and she had to have had help. His possessiveness roared at the thought of another person seeing her like this, so he had to quickly suppress that reaction. It was probably one of her girlfriends, and she did it with him in mind.

He had to get his wits about him. She did this for him, but he wanted to make sure she enjoyed every minute of it. Just as he fully intended to. Her pleasure was bonded to his, and he wanted to make this good for both of them. As his resolve settled in, another emotion drove forward.

Dominance.

Ian felt it overcome his senses. He didn't

care. Cassie knew his kinks and had already been exposed to that aspect of his sex life. He wouldn't resist the temptation to embrace it now.

"Who helped you, Cassie?" His voice was so guttural he barely recognized it as his own.

"Sasha."

"Hmmm." He was relieved that his suspicion was accurate. "Where is she?"

"Um, in the living room, I think."

Perfect. "Roll on your side," he ordered.

She struggled within her bindings to do as he requested, but there was enough slack to accommodate her maneuverings. If he'd tied her up, she wouldn't be able to budge, but this worked for what he needed. When she finished, she was panting from her efforts. And maybe from anticipation, he'd like to think.

Cassie didn't say anything. The thought that she was waiting for his command made pride swell inside him. His woman was giving him this control. Why wouldn't he be proud and honored by her gift?

Drawing out her anticipation, he picked up his BlackBerry and searched his contacts. He glanced at Cassie's face and saw her brow furrow in confusion, but she still didn't say anything. He selected the person he wanted to call and put the phone up to his ear, his eyes still on Cassie.

"Hello?"

"Sasha?" Cassie's eyes grew when she realized he'd called her accomplice. Ian kept his expression neutral. "Can you come into Cassie's bedroom?"

"You finished already?" There was a hint of amusement in her voice, thinking he was done with Cassie. Oh, he wasn't done with her. Not now, not ever. He felt shocked at that realization and mentally shook it off.

"Not yet. I need your help. That is if you don't mind a little hands-on action." He'd give her the option.

Sasha hesitated. "Er, okay. Be right in."

Ian disconnected the call and watched Cassie. She opened her mouth but snapped it shut when he gave her a reprimanding look. This type of relationship required trust, so she'd have to trust him to see to their pleasure. He preferred no one else look at her like this, but since Cassie was comfortable with Sasha seeing her exposed, he could use Sasha for what he needed.

He heard Cassie's bedroom door open and saw her head crane around to look at Sasha. She didn't come into view.

"Keep your eyes on me, baby."

Cassie reluctantly looked at him, and he figured Sasha was trying to communicate with Cassie without his knowledge. The fact Sasha was probably trying to make sure

Cassie was all right with this made him respect her friend a little more.

Sasha walked to the side of the bed, displaying a sense of sexual prowess that seemed a little forced to be fully true. "My, my, my, I do declare that is one big cock, Mr. Cope."

He stroked it, not taking his eyes off his possession. What Sasha thought of him didn't matter. He was only focused on the goddess on the bed. "Cassie has been a bad little girl. I need you to see to her punishment."

Cassie's eyes flickered to Sasha and back to the screen. "Baby, I told you to keep your eyes on me. You're already gonna be spanked for letting another person see you like this. You don't want extra lashes for disobedience."

Sasha laughed. "You want me to spank her for surprising you?" At that, he looked at Sasha, and she was shaking her head. "You're a coldhearted bastard." She stuck her tongue out, licking her lips, and cocked her head to the side. "Or one kinky son of a bitch."

He winked at her and turned his attention back to Cassie. No way in hell was he seriously punishing her for doing this for him. He just wanted to push her a little, see if she'd let him call the shots. It wasn't as if he was there and could unleash his dominance himself. God, he'd give anything to be the person marking her ass. He'd just have to live vicariously though Sasha right now. "Use your hand, Sasha. Don't stop until I tell you to."

She threw Cassie a look of *you asked for this* and landed the first blow. Cassie yelped and twisted her body but didn't take her eyes off Ian.

"Stay still, baby." Sasha swatted Cassie again, and she complied. "Good girl," he murmured.

Seeming to accept what she was actually doing, Sasha released a barrage of smacks, alternating cheeks. Ian groaned, fisting his cock while he watched Cassie whimpering with panting breaths. Her face was flushed, eyes glazed with arousal.

And Sasha kept them coming, driving up his and Cassie's desire. He couldn't take much more of this.

"Enough," he ordered. "You can leave."

Without preamble, Sasha walked away, and he heard the door shut.

"You know how fucking hot that was watching a woman spank what's mine?"

She groaned, her legs parting, the evidence of her arousal coating her thighs.

"Roll over and show me your ass."

Cassie moved around, and when her buttocks came into view, he growled at how beautiful it looked. The rosy blooms of Sasha's handprint inflamed Cassie's backside. Jesus, he wanted to feel the heat coming off it.

"Lie on your back and spread your legs for me, baby."

As she struggled to get supine, he opened the browser that contained the controls to her dildo. Once she was in position, Ian selected the lowest setting, watching her hips wiggle as she took what he dished out. He played with her, leaving it on the lowest setting for a while, listening to her murmurs of approval because it felt good, of protest since he wouldn't up the intensity. He rubbed his cock harder, faster as he watched her writhe on the bed. Then he upped the setting and she squealed.

"Oh God, Ian."

"You like that, baby?"

He knew he did. He didn't give her a chance to answer. He increased it again, watching her get closer to her orgasm. A few seconds later, she shouted, "I'm gonna come!"

He turned off the device and she gasped in confusion, looking around the room and then settling her gaze on him. She pouted as her head fell back to the pillow.

"You'll come when I'm ready for you to, Cassie."

He continued his torment of her. And his torment of himself, because by denying her climax he was denying his. He brought her to the edge and yanked her back several times over the next hour. He'd worked his cock with the same torturous action, enduring the pain of his near orgasms for the pleasure he would finally achieve when they went over together.

When she was a blubbering, sensitive mess, ready to go off as soon as he tried changing his ministrations, she was the most beautiful thing he'd even seen. His own body was overheated, heart racing, sweat pouring down his face, chest. He'd have thought he was beyond any cognitive processes, but seeing her spread before him, he couldn't help but think he wanted to be with her. Not only possess her in reality but cherish her, love her.

He groaned at the bombardment of emotions swarming him and hit the highest setting on Cassie's vibrator as he pumped his cock with relentless abandon. He barely registered her crying out his name over the roar of the blood rushing in his head. He shouted his own release and shivered at how painful the pleasure actually was. His orgasm went on forever, and when it finally ebbed, he shut off the vibrator and slumped over, spent.

He was losing himself to her, and he had no idea what to do about that.

CHAPTER NINE

Cassie stepped out of the supply closet Monday afternoon with her phone in hand, trying to suppress her heavy panting.

"Looking for new pens?" Sasha asked from behind Cassie, and she whirled.

"Um, er, I, ah."

Her phone buzzed and she looked guiltily at it.

"Oh my God! You were having phone sex in the supply room?" Sasha whispered. "I swear you two are like rabbits."

She was right. But after Cassie's surprise Friday night, something had changed in this *thing* between Ian and her. He hadn't wanted to disconnect after their mind-blowing sex. Sasha had freed Cassie before escaping, but then she and Ian had stayed up half the night talking. They'd spent the weekend chatting online, talking on the phone and even having a movie night last night. They'd both watched the same movie on HBO, ate popcorn and talked the evening away before submerging themselves in heated passion well into the night. They'd had lots of sex over the weekend, but it was different, more emotional.

"For goodness' sake, you haven't even kissed the man!" Sasha all but laughed. "I can't get into a relationship with a guy without knowing if he's a good kisser."

Cassie shrugged as she uselessly adjusted her shirt and headed back to her desk. "This is different."

"You, girl, are falling for him like a ton of bricks."

"So?" Cassie mumbled.

Sasha sighed and tugged at Cassie's arm so she'd look up. "Just be careful. There are company rules about this kind of stuff. And I don't want you getting hurt."

"There are rules about letting a man watch me masturbate?" Cassie asked with false innocence.

Sasha smirked. "Technicality, my dear. Anyway, just play it cool."

"Yes, Mother." Cassie rolled her eyes. "Just so you know, Ian and I finished up our work on the project this morning, acceptance testing successfully completed and documentation finalized. We signed off on everything, and now he's on his way to a meeting with his boss to close out the assignment. So there.

We didn't let our personal lives interfere with our work."

Sasha gave her a placating look. "I never said you'd botch your job for a little dick action." After they both chuckled, Sasha sobered. "What happens now that your project is over?"

Cassie hadn't wanted to think about that. Logically, she knew they'd go their separate ways. This was just a little digital romance, and now that their project was finished, it didn't make sense to continue it. Ian lived out west, and Cassie knew it wouldn't be healthy to carry on seeing him like this. It'd just keep her from getting out there and having real dates with men who could actually touch her.

So why did her heart ache each time she thought about calling it quits? She didn't really have to ask herself that question. She knew the truth. She was falling in love with him, and the more time she spent with him, the faster she was falling. What was she going to do about him?

"I don't know," she finally answered. Because deep down, that was the only answer that made any sense.

———

IAN SAT at the conference room table with Mac and the bigwigs that'd flown in this morning. He sat, facing what felt like his executioners. He knew he wasn't losing his job, but Cassie was going to, and he was so attached to her now that he felt as if this were happening to him. And he felt like shit for his hand being forced in her downfall.

After his personal meeting with Mac yesterday afternoon, Ian had given Cassie a lame excuse about having plans with his brother last night and had spent the evening getting drunk.

His hangover didn't help his self-reproaching woes this morning.

He was an asshole. There was no bigger asshole than him. Regardless of how he felt about engaging in a digital relationship with Cassie in the beginning—it was something new to try with a woman he'd had a thing for—it turned out to be so much more. In this relationship he expected her to trust him to see to her sexual needs. But those were the only needs he sought to protect. And in that, he was a hypocrite. She'd given him all her trust. She hadn't rationed it out, only giving it to him in one aspect of her life. She trusted him fully. And what had he done? He hadn't trusted her enough to open up about what he had to do. It didn't matter that Mac told him to keep quiet about her office closing. He should have been honest with her.

"We're pleased you were able to stop by

before your trip to the other offices," Mac said to the executives at the table.

They all chitchatted as everyone settled down and prepared for the meeting ahead.

"Mr. Winthrop, Mr. Cartwright, Mrs. Downing, I hope you've had an opportunity to view the consolidation plan Ian Cope has prepared via directive from me regarding the initiative to consolidate the southern office I've been overseeing," Mac stated as he glanced at Ian in recognition. He was a little surprised by that. He didn't want any part of this mess, but it was unlike Mac to share any glory, no matter how bloody the battle.

"We have, and we agree with the assessment. Closing that office will save millions and increase our cash flow, which is needed for the new direction of our software products. Did you build the generic prototype we want to market to the security industry?" Mr. Winthrop asked.

"Yes sir." Mac pulled up the application on the overhead projector and showed how seamlessly it could be modified to fit individual client needs. He droned on and on while Ian shifted uncomfortably in his seat.

He had to do something. He owed it to Cassie to try to save her job, but these jokers were only interested in the bottom line, and it really did make sense to close that location. It didn't matter, though. He would try something. When the conversation drifted back to the office closure and off new product development, Ian found his window.

"With the level of expertise in the southern office on this particular application, it might make sense to consider keeping a few members onboard," Ian said thoughtfully. Or he hoped like hell he sounded that way, because he really felt desperate.

Mac immediately looked irritated and bustled to respond. "If you felt that way, Cope, you should've outlined that in your consolidation plan."

Not taking the bait, Ian sat up straighter. "I agree closing that office makes the most sense. But with the influx of clients we expect with the launch of this new application, it seems logical to keep some of the talent who initially created it."

"Yes, well, your office modified it. There's no need to keep any of the old team members," Mr. Cartwright said as he poured a glass of water from the complimentary pitcher.

His office modified it? What about the joint effort with the other office. What about Cassie's work? "Mr. Cartwright, I don't think you understand. This office—"

"Easily finished the assignment assigned to it," Mac finished, cutting off Ian's explanation. He glanced at his immediate supervisor, and Mac was glaring daggers at him.

Mr. Cartwright stood, followed by the

other two. "We need to be on our way, we have a meeting with Mr. Weiner this afternoon. We have an office to close."

The three ill-informed executives quickly left the room, but Ian wasn't watching them, he was staring down Mac.

"What *the fuck* was that about?" he asked once the coast was clear.

"We had an application to build, and you needed to create a consolidation plan. We didn't need their help on the software changes. It was only a ruse to get in to do your real job."

"And that's why you didn't want anyone else over there working on it. You didn't want to risk the chance of that office getting any credit." Mac was a fucking weasel!

"It's a sinking ship, Cope. You know it. I know it. There's no need to draw praise when it'll fall on deaf ears."

Ian slammed his hands down on the table. "That's bullshit! I'm going to clear this up right now!"

Mac stepped forward, blocking his exit. "You do that, and you're fired. You were given an order, and you followed it. I can't help it if they want to close that office. This is just business. It's not my fault you crossed the line and got involved with Cassie Tucker."

The blood drained from Ian's face. How the hell did Mac know about that?

"Don't look so surprised. You've been looking for a reason to work with her for years. Of course you're involved with her. I just hope you were smart enough not to leave a trail. We have a policy about office romance. Your texts and emails on company equipment are property of the company." Mac gave Ian a knowing look, but Ian and Cassie had been careful. Sure, there were a few innuendos made on company cell phones and emails, but the hot-and-heavy stuff happened through personal equipment.

Ignoring the comment about Cassie, Ian glared at Mac. "You can't fire me for doing my job. I have every right to inform the executive staff about the south regional office's involvement in the product modification."

"But I can fire you for becoming involved with Cassie Tucker." Mac sighed. "You made the mistake of getting too personal, Cope. Leave this alone. Don't make that same mistake now."

How could he not? He betrayed the woman he loved.

Loved?

Shit shit shit shit!

Oh, yeah, he was definitely the biggest asshole who walked the face of the Earth.

———

CASSIE GRABBED her notebook and hustled into the conference room with the rest of the office. She didn't know what all the hubbub was about. Like everyone else, she'd seen the top executives in here talking to Richard and other upper management. It wasn't a common occurrence to see them all here, but it wasn't necessarily uncommon, either. A couple of times a year, they'd descend and gab about quarterly profits with a speech about teamwork driving the company into the future. The same speech probably every executive at every company had given to peons across the nation.

But what was odd was that they hadn't spoken to the entire office, only the managers, and then they'd left.

That was only fifteen minutes ago, and immediately meeting notifications went out to everyone. People were speculating left and right on what this could be about. Some were speculating about a raise. Others were less optimistic.

Cassie was in the latter group. She didn't believe for one second that if it were good news, the executives wouldn't want to tell everybody themselves.

By the time she got into the meeting it was standing room only. The conference table only seated about twenty and there were forty in the office.

"Marks, shut the door," Richard said over the murmurs across the room as Sophie

Marks walked in. She was so pregnant that she waddled. The woman was ridiculously adorable, and Cassie was going to miss her dearly when she went on maternity leave.

She was surprised the woman hadn't gone on leave already.

After shutting the door, Sophie took a seat closest to it, and Richard turned his attention to the congregated group. "There is no easy way to say this, so I'll just come out with it. Our office is closing."

Cassie shut her eyes as her stomach plummeted. The buzz of voices picked up again as panic set in. Several people barked questions concerning why and when—including the very pregnant Sophie at the end of the table—but Cassie couldn't understand enough to even find words.

This was her first job out of college. She'd worked here for years, moving up the ladder. She had a mortgage, a car payment, credit card bills, student loans... She was going to be sick.

"I know this is a shock to everyone. The company is doing well, and they are impressed with the work we've done. But they are redefining our, er, I mean, their marketing strategy." He cleared his throat and looked down while he took a fortifying breath. Richard was obviously taking this hard too. Then he looked at everyone again. "We close our doors at the end of the month. Everyone's severance package is based on years of service. Look in the manual or your employment contracts to determine what you're entitled to. Please let me know if you have any questions. The company will provide employment counseling and replacement assistance for anyone interested."

Yeah, like she'd ask for help from the shitheads who'd throw her out without a second thought. Cassie had worked her ass off for this company. Hell, she'd just finished a major project that probably helped with the company's new focus. And did they care? Apparently not. She and Ian had worked hard on that.

Ian.

Shit! Was it just this office closing down, or was his office on the chopping block too? She'd have to call him and tell him what happened, hoping he was in the clear. Cassie looked around, and her colleagues were at different stages of grief. Most were still too shocked to process what was happening, some fuming mad, others crying. She wasn't crying yet. But when she looked at Sasha, she felt the first pang of sadness. Sasha was stuck between shocked and crying. Cassie had to go to her, console her. She was on her way over when Richard adjourned the meeting.

"Tucker?" he called to her. She stopped and turned to him as the room cleared out. Sasha stayed frozen in place.

"Yes?"

"Did Cope mention anything to you about this?"

Confused, Cassie looked at him. "No. Why would he?"

"Evidently, he was the one who created the consolidation plan to close this office. He presented it to the executives this morning."

Cassie felt her knees give and grabbed the edge of the table, bracing herself. Her head was spinning, blackness surrounding her. No! This was impossible. She wouldn't, couldn't believe this. She started shaking her head before she could find her voice.

"He and Mac met with them. When I asked about your work on this project, they said nothing was mentioned to them about it."

Too many emotions swamped her. Anger, betrayal, devastation, they all hurt. Richard kept talking, but she couldn't hear the words anymore. Her eyes watered. She wasn't crying before. She was crying now. Sasha stepped over, a look of regret marring her normally spunky face. She felt sorry for Cassie, and Cassie was too lost to fully register her friend's pity. Her phone vibrated since she'd turned the ringer off for the meeting. She numbly pulled it out of her pocket and stared at Ian's number. She sobbed at the instant stab to her heart. He'd used her. He didn't feel anything for her. It was just another day at the office. At the next buzz, she accepted the call and put the phone to her ear. She didn't know why she did that. It wasn't as if she could talk right now. She tried to say hello but she couldn't catch her breath to speak.

"Oh God, baby, let me explain," Ian pleaded.

Cassie ended the call, threw the phone like it'd bitten her, and collapsed into the chair beside her. Her head fell into her hands and she wept.

The man she loved had used her.

She wanted to die.

CHAPTER TEN

By Friday, Cassie was too numb to feel anything. She stayed in bed, only getting out to fix a bowl of ice cream when she got tired of pretzels, which stayed by the bed. She never realized one could live off eating only those two things, but she was a living case study. She considered starting a blog about it. Maybe she could do that for a living since she needed a new job. She loved her some ice cream. She could focus on new flavors of ice cream and varying brands of pretzels each week, concentrating on the nutritional aspect of carbs. Yeah, that'd go over really well, she thought as she crumbled up some pretzels as an impromptu topping for her rocky road.

She hadn't shown up at work since the big announcement. What would they do? Fire her some more? She was already an elite member of the unemployment club. She had the snazzy new t-shirt and everything. But she knew she had to clean out her desk. She figured she'd go in sometime next week to do that. She didn't see the rush in pounding the last nail into that coffin.

After she'd hung up the phone on Ian that afternoon, Richard had told her his belief that Ian had pumped information out of Cassie to complete his report. That theory was surely floating around the office, with her coworkers hating her guts by now. She couldn't really blame them. They needed something to focus their frustrations on, and she made the perfect scapegoat. Cassie knew it wasn't her fault the company administration made this call, but she also knew she'd played an unwitting part in the demise of her colleagues' careers. And she just couldn't face everyone yet.

That was her clinical observation. She couldn't allow her emotional observation to be considered, because as soon as she thought about what Ian had done, what this meant to her heart, she would start crying all over again. So she steeled herself against the pain. Being numb was better than thinking about what he did.

A knock sounded at her door and she groaned into her ice cream, ignoring the visitor. She didn't want to speak to anyone. And by God, she wasn't going to.

"Damn it, girl, I know you're in there.

Open this door!" Sasha yelled from the other side as she pounded relentlessly.

"Shit," Cassie groaned as she made her way to the front of her house, and when she got there, she yanked the door open. "I have neighbors, for crying out loud! What do you want?"

"Well, now, is that any way to treat your comrade? Go get dressed." She stepped past Cassie, walking into her house. "Strike that. Go scrub your stinkin' ass first, then get dressed. Tonight we're hittin' the bar."

"I don't wanna go out," Cassie mumbled as she closed the door and followed.

Sasha leveled her stare directly on Cassie. "I didn't ask."

"Damn it, Sasha. I don't feel like it."

"You listen to me, Cass. You owe me big-time, remember? Just because that traitorous prick is on your shit list now doesn't negate the fact I spanked your ass for him. It's time to start paying up, and you going out with me tonight is a good start."

Cassie sighed, defeated. Sasha did go way above and beyond the call of girlfriend duty, and Cassie always repaid her friends. "Give me thirty minutes." She turned to walk away.

"Take an hour, because damn, you look rough."

After Cassie showered, shaved, plucked and buffed her way back to the land of the living, she put on the ridiculously sexy outfit her friend had picked out. This hooker dress counted as part of paying back her debt. She was keeping score.

Sasha drove to the bar, intending on getting Cassie too drunk to drive herself home. She was fine with that. Alcohol had amazing numbing powers. She'd have indulged more these last few days if liquor and ice cream went better together. She didn't mind giving her ice cream the night off.

When they walked in, the music was blaring and bodies were gyrating. Cassie tuned it all out and made a beeline for the bar. Sasha followed her, yelling two drink orders while Cassie fiddled around in her purse.

"You look beautiful tonight," a male voice said as her drink was placed in front of her. She looked up and right into Chip's eyes. Crap. She sort of forgotten about him. She glanced over at Sasha, who was doing a piss-poor job of hiding her smile. Ugh! Cassie just realized she was much slower grasping the meaning of tonight. This was just a ploy Sasha orchestrated to get Cassie to see Chip. Her friend was one dead bitch.

"Thanks." She smiled, and he nodded as he walked away, working on another drink order. Her smile faded as she turned to Sasha. "This favor counts as more than just a simple night-on-the-town favor."

"I. Spanked. Your. Ass. The only way we'll be even anytime soon is if you take lover boy over there to the back room, lift up your dress and let him stick his dick inside you."

Cassie snorted as she tried to take a drink. "How do you figure me getting laid would even the score between us?"

"Because I'd gladly call us square if you'd take one for the team. Ain't nothing wrong with some causal lovin'. Besides, Chip is a cutie patootie."

Cassie took a big gulp of her martini. Damn, he made it ever better than last time. "I'm through with men for a while, Sasha."

Sasha waved at Chip when Cassie set her empty glass down. He quickly prepared her another and placed it in front of her. He wasn't making small talk, and she figured he was keeping his distance because she'd rejected him last time. She was relieved he wasn't making another attempt tonight. She really didn't have the strength to fight off advances right now.

The girls chatted about work, or lack thereof, for most of the evening. By the time Cassie was on her fourth drink and Sasha had just started nursing her second, Cassie was feeling much better. She should've given more consideration to the alcohol-versus-ice-cream argument earlier in the week. Booze rocked!

"Hey, Chip," Cassie slurred. "I'm hungry."

He eyed her briefly before walking over. Sasha gave him an apologetic look. "Whatcha got to eat?"

"Kitchen's still open. You can have whatever you want. I'll grab you some menus."

Cassie grabbed his arm as he started to walk off. "I just want a cheeeeseburger. Oh, and, er, fries, yeah. No wait, onion rings. Just don't bring me any pretzels or ice cream. I looove ice cream, but I can't, I need something else to eat now." She kept hold of his arm, staring at him.

"Cheeseburger and rings. No ice cream or pretzels. Got it." He pulled at his arm, but she wouldn't let go. Wow, he felt really strong. She stared at his muscular forearm, fascinated. "I need you to let go, babe, so I can get your food," he murmured.

"'Kaaay." She let go and he turned to Sasha.

"I'll have the same."

He nodded and walked away, and Cassie started eating the olives out of her martini. When Chip brought the girls their food, Cassie still had a little left in her glass.

"I need another one of these things." Cassie picked up her glass and tilted it from side to side as if it were empty. Chip steadied her hand and helped her set it back down.

"You still have a little left. I'll make you one when you're ready."

Sasha cleared her throat, but Cassie didn't give a care what she was hinting at when she shook her head at Chip. "We, er, lost our jobs this week."

Chip slumped down, leaning against the bar. "I'm sorry to hear that," he said, facing Sasha first and then Cassie. "You okay?"

Cassie shrugged as she tried to take a bite of her burger. When she swallowed the small amount, she looked up at him. "Why are men such fucking assholes?"

He laughed through a shocked expression. Her comment had totally caught him off guard. "I don't know, babe. But we can be bastards sometimes."

Cassie munched on an onion ring. "I mean, wouldn't you like it if I tied myself to the bed and let Sasha spank my ass for your viewing pleasure?"

"Cassie!" Sasha winced, but Cassie waved her off, feeling somewhat unbalanced by the maneuver.

"I'd watch any chick spank that fine ass of yours," some guy sitting next to Cassie said as she wobbled into him.

She leaned on the balding, middle-aged man. "Awww, now, you're sweet."

He reached up and patted her back, letting his hand linger. Chip scowled. "Hands off, man. She asked me that question."

The guy lifted his hands innocently and then went back to his beer. Chip leaned on the bar, glancing back and forth between Sasha and Cassie. "You let her do that?" he whispered with a smile.

"Uh-huh." She took another bite of her burger. "That's why guys are such dickheads. They get you off and then get you fired," she mumbled around a full mouth. Then she downed the rest of her martini. "I need more."

"I'll get you some water."

"I don't want—" She turned to look at Sasha. "He just walked away."

"Eat your burger. Then he might fix you another martini."

Cassie was swallowing another bite when Chip walked over with her water. She frowned but didn't argue. She ate about half of her burger and rings and drank all of her water. "*Chiiiiip*," Cassie called out. He walked over to her. "I-I finished my food and my water. I want c'nother martini now. Sasha drives me home tonight."

"How about I make you a martini and you tell me about your week?"

She grudgingly nodded. She didn't really want to rehash everything, but if it got her more alcohol, she'd comply.

Chip walked back over, handing Cassie her drink. "I even put extra olives in it for you."

"Oooh, yummy. I love olives." She immediately started eating them as Chip mumbled something to Sasha about some virgin something-or-other.

"So tell me about your week," he pressed.

Cassie mumbled the tale, stumbling through the details, and leaned on Sasha to help fill in when she either got too tired or too confused to continue. This alcohol stuff was great but really messed with her concentration. By the time she'd finished, she was crashing from her buzz. Oh, she was drunk as a skunk, but reliving the nightmare of this past week was a major downer. She laid her head on the bar, trying to fight the emotions coming over her. When Chip stroked her hair, she had to fight the tears. His touch was so gentle.

And so real.

There wasn't a computer monitor or a phone screen between them. She needed to get out of here before she did something she'd regret. Leaving her head on the bar, Cassie turned to Sasha. "I'm ready to go home now. Can you pull the car up to the door, so I don't have to walk far?"

"Sure thing, girl."

Sasha hopped down, and Cassie sat up, the sudden movement making her bladder scream. How many drinks did she have anyway? She slid off the stool and realized she didn't remember how to work her feet. It was a strange feeling knowing she was too drunk to walk but thinking she could pretend she was fine. She looked up at Chip, and he had a concerned look on his face, arms braced as if he were ready to run around to her. "Where's the bathroom?"

"It's down the hall." He pointed to the left, and Cassie mentally gauged the three hundred miles she'd have to walk to get there. She looked at Chip again.

"Can you help me?"

"Sure. Stay right there." He walked over to her and wrapped his arm around her waist. "C'mon, babe." He gently walked her to the bathroom and helped her in. Then he stood outside while she took care of her business. When she was finished, he helped her out. "I'm sorry you had such a bad week," he whispered.

Cassie stopped and looked up at him. They stared at each other in the narrow hall, the music muffled by the doors blocking the entrance. She reached up and stroked his cheek, which went hard as he gritted his teeth. She knew this wasn't the man she loved. She just wanted someone to take the pain away.

Leaning up, she brushed her lips across his. When he didn't open for her, she licked the seam, probing for entry. He groaned, opening up for her invasion. After a few seconds, he slid his hands into her hair and kissed her back. When Cassie shut her eyes, it wasn't Chip she saw. It wasn't Chip who kissed her so passionately. And it wasn't Chip she wrapped her arms around and clung to.

He broke away, gasping into her hair. "Cassie, babe, you're hurting, and you're drunk. I can't take advantage of your vulnerability like that. Not like this." He pulled away and guided her out of the bar and helped her into the car.

Why couldn't she have fallen in love with Chip? He was a good guy. He didn't want to hurt her. He was obviously attracted to her, but he put her needs above his own.

And yet she tried to use him to take away the pain of what Ian had done to her.

How did that make her any better than Ian?

CHAPTER ELEVEN

THE WORLD LOOKED different when one was hungover. The soft light filtering in through the curtains felt like looking directly into the blazing sun. The birds chirping merrily sounded like hawks screeching while in attack mode, circling their prey.

Cassie didn't remember much after her third martini. Why did her breath smell like onions? She should've stuck with ice cream and pretzels. She crawled out of bed, her back howling in protest as she tried to move. She had to brush her teeth. If she continued to taste onions, she'd puke.

She just might puke anyway.

Holy crap, she looked like a horror beauty queen. Her hair was stuck to the side of her face, and mascara ran halfway down her cheeks. She quickly brushed her teeth, trying to ignore her revolting stomach. Then she crept to the shower to clean up the mess that was her face and hair. Too bad she couldn't find an easy fix to clean up her life. Thank God her head was pounding too much for her to continue down that train of thought.

When she got dressed, she decided to take advantage of it being Saturday and go clean out her desk. The only time anyone worked on the weekends was during major deadlines or kissing up for promotions. She highly doubted anybody was feeling overly eager to put in extra time nowadays.

She stopped for coffee because she needed some serious caffeine and called Sasha to get the skinny on what went down last night. After the initial hellos and Cassie telling Sasha she was going to clean out her desk, Cassie braced herself for the information she sought. To her total embarrassment, Sasha relayed every humiliating detail up until she went to get the car. Then she snickered.

"Chip brought you out, and he was acting a little peculiar. I would've asked what happened, but after he fastened your seatbelt, you leaned over and kissed him before passing out. I took it by his reaction that it wasn't the first time you'd done that."

"Oh God, I kissed him!"

"Big, wet, moaning, sloppy kiss. Gotta say, it made me want to spank your ass again." She laughed. "Maybe we should just be lesbians. Who needs men?"

She joked to ease Cassie's mortification. It wasn't working. She wasn't able to stop the agonizing moan that escaped her lips.

"Hey, hey, stop that wounded-animal sound. He looked over at me and told me to tell you not to feel guilty about a damn thing. I promise that's what he said. Then he wanted me to let you know that you can give him a call when you were ready." She paused. "He knows you're heartbroken right now, and he's seriously interested in you."

"I wish it were that simple, Sasha."

"I know you fell hard, girl. You'll get over that dickhead, and when you do, you'll waltz into that bar and claim another man."

As handsome and nice as Chip was, Cassie still couldn't bring herself to think of him—or any other man—in that way. Only one man would do it for her. She sighed hopelessly. "Would I have to eat your pussy if we tried out this lesbian thing?"

Sasha made a choking sound. "Eww, gross. How 'bout we stick to dildos and only touch ourselves? I still need some dick if I'm going to play with a girl."

"Then we'd just be masturbating in front of each other, and I think I'm good on that." She tried to joke, but the memories of doing that with Ian were too painful right now. She pulled into the parking lot as she tried clearing her head. "I'm here. I'll talk to you later."

"Bye, girl. Call me if you need anything."

Cassie hung up and walked into the building. It felt very surreal being here, knowing this wasn't her job anymore. She guessed if she didn't want to burn this bridge as her only job reference, she'd better officially put in some kind of notice. Just walking out with her tail tucked between her legs without any kind of word to her boss was unprofessional. She really hated taking the high road. Thoughts of uprooting all the plants and turning off the air conditioner in the server room crossed her mind. A little evil laugh made her feel better. Ah, if only she were a vindictive person.

She made her way to her desk and booted up her computer. At least they hadn't disabled her network account yet. She figured Richard was hoping she'd be back next week. He'd be wrong. She opened her email and saw the hundreds of messages. Ugh! She sorted them by name and only read the ones from her boss, which were all work related. She had several in there from Ian, but she just couldn't read them. She was a coward. So what?

She submitted leave for the time she was out last week and a vacation request for the rest of the month. She was just going to resign early, but she wasn't sure what that'd do to her severance package. Those shitheads would be paying her for the six months they owed her. If her vacation time was denied, she'd reevaluate her circumstances.

Cassie cleaned out her desk, shredding old paperwork that nobody needed, and packed up her personal belongings. When she was finished, her desk resembled many others around her. It looked as if she wasn't the only scorned employee who didn't want to stick around for the guillotine. As she picked up her box, she noticed her message button blinking on her phone. She stared at it and considered listening to them all, but she knew at least one, if not a lot, of those would be from Ian. If she couldn't bring herself to read his emails, no way was she able to listen to his voice. Besides, if any of the messages were work related, it really didn't matter. She clutched her box tighter and strode purposely toward the front door, never looking back.

She felt really proud of herself. She didn't cry until she was on the freeway, but once she started, she bawled uncontrollably. She'd kept her feelings numb, not allowing herself to grieve for what she'd truly lost, and now those emotions were pouring out of her. She pulled over onto the shoulder and buried her head in her hands, letting the tears fall. After she cried for a while, she figured she needed to get home before someone pulled over and checked on her. People were kind in the South. They did that sort of thing. Gathering her inner strength, she wiped her eyes and merged onto the road. Her breath was hitching and her eyes were sore and swollen, but she only thought about the road to home.

When she pulled up into her driveway, there was a large SUV parked to the side. Crap, she didn't want company right now. She looked like shit. She didn't recognize the vehicle and the windows were tinted. Oh well. She slid out of her car and grabbed her box. Whoever it was would just have to deal with her like this. When she walked up her sidewalk, the driver-side door opened, and a man got out. She did a double take when his profile was partially covered from the tall vehicle he was getting out of. She saw disheveled brown hair and sunglasses. When he turned and headed straight for her, she gasped and her body froze.

Ian.

The air locked in her lungs. She couldn't breathe. She. Could. Not. Breathe! Her body started shaking as she stared at him openmouthed. Open, because she hoped the air would find its way to her lungs on its own since she'd forgotten the mechanics of that bodily function.

He stopped in front of her and slid his sunglasses to rest on top of his head. His eyes were agonized as he looked at her.

"Cassie," he breathed, her name a benediction. He swallowed, cleared his throat and started to say something but also looked as if he were waiting for some kind of acknowledgment from her.

"You're tall," she muttered. Why did she start with that? Must be the nerves.

His somber eyes twinkled briefly at her comment. He shoved his hands in his pockets and rocked on his heels. "Told you I was."

She nodded and stared, dumbfounded. She knew she had a lot to say to him. They'd never talked about what happened. Shouldn't she be screaming at him and telling him to get lost? Yeah, she'd do that. She just needed to work up to that point.

"I, um... Can I come in?"

"Er, sure." She nodded as she started to turn and then gasped when Ian reached out for the box. Their fingertips touched, his lingering before pulling the box from her grasp.

She dug out her keys as she walked to the door with him following closely behind. Her heart was racing and now she was breathing much too fast. If she didn't slow it down, she'd pass out. They walked in, and she turned on the lights while he set her stuff on the table. He glanced around, taking in their surroundings, then took a deep breath as he faced her. She felt like a feeble kitten standing in front of a vicious Rottweiler. Helpless as his gaze zeroed in on her. Oh he didn't look ferocious. Far from it. He looked almost as bad as she did. The only reason she looked worse was because she'd just recently bawled like a baby over losing her job. Losing him.

And now he was standing in her living room.

"I'm sorry," he said, shutting his eyes. She shook her head and stepped away from him. She didn't know if she could have this conversation in person. He followed her. "I know it doesn't even begin to make up for the damage and pain I caused you."

She turned on him then. "Why?" she barked. "Why did you do this to me? Why didn't you tell me?"

He raised his hands in a playacting gesture. "You have every right to be mad—"

"Don't you fucking patronize me!" She advanced on him, poking her finger in his chest. "You came all the way out here to speak your mind, so you better start. You don't get to tell me what I do and don't have a right to feel."

He grabbed her wrists and yanked her up against his chest to stop her assault. "I'm sorry. You're right. I fucked up big time. I was ordered to do that consolidation report, to pump you for information and to keep quiet about it. I used you, and I hated it. I'm sorry."

She pulled her arms free, stepping away from him. It was hard enough looking at him. She couldn't deal with his touch. She'd fantasized about those hands caressing her, wondering what they'd feel like on her skin. Now she knew the soft yet calloused feel. She seared that experience into her brain and knew she'd always remember how hot his hands felt on her body. Had he not tortured her enough already?

"What are you doing here?" she asked, folding her arms across her chest. She would not cry. She would not cry. She would not cry. If she told herself that enough times, maybe the tears welling in her eyes would just evaporate.

He stepped up to her and rubbed his hand down the length of her arm. Damn him! Why was he touching her? God, it felt so good. Her breath caught in an effort to stave off any crying she was about to do. He leaned in, his head resting on the side of her head, his lips by her ear.

"I love you," he whispered.

She shook her head in denial and tried pushing him away. He grabbed both her arms and held her tightly against him.

"Don't push me away, Cassie. Please just let me get this out. Then if you want me to leave, I will."

He rubbed his head in her hair. She trembled. He was everywhere, pressed against her, breathing on her. She'd never forget any of this. She couldn't believe he felt about her the way she felt about him. It wasn't possible.

He just felt guilty. His arms wrapped around her, one hand fisting in her hair as he groaned into her ear. Her knees buckled and his hold tightened.

"I've got you," he said softly, meaning he'd stopped her from falling, but then he repeated it over and over again, the meaning clearly changing.

"Ian..." She didn't know what to say. She shouldn't let him touch her like this.

His lips found the sensitive spot below her ear, and she was a goner. The hurt he'd caused didn't matter anymore. She'd been more intimate with this man than she'd ever been with any other. Without ever having touched him. She couldn't fight the need boiling inside her now. This contact was all she'd ever dreamed about, and after everything that'd happened between them, she at least wanted this dream fulfilled.

She moaned as his lips caressed the column of her neck, and he took that as an invitation. His hands tangled in her hair, and his mouth crashed onto hers. Her surprised gasp gave him direct access to the wet heat he sought. His tongue plundered, exploring every crevice and dueling with hers. Ian was kissing her. She'd lain awake at night and visualized what this would be like.

She never dreamed it'd be this good.

She pulled away to breathe, and he kissed and nipped at her neck. When she buried her fingers in his hair and pulled him back to her lips, he groaned and kissed her again, squatting down and lifting her into his arms.

"Your room?" he asked between kisses while walking down the only hallway. She pointed aimlessly, but he found it. He kicked the door closed as he strode to the bed, setting her down beside it. He continued kissing her while they frantically toed off shoes and tugged and pulled at each other's clothing, only breaking away to pull their shirts free. When they were both naked, he pulled away, caressing her face with his hands while he caressed her body with his gaze. "You're so beautiful, baby." He picked her up and laid her on the bed. "You don't know how many times I dreamed about actually being in this room with you."

Oh, she could only guess it was as many times as she'd envisioned being in his.

Ian crawled onto the bed above her. His tall, toned frame hovered over. He supported his weight with one arm, barely touching her, as his lips found her nipple. She cried out when he bit it lovingly and suckled it, drawing it to the roof of his mouth, his free hand finding the other one.

He alternated kissing, sucking one nipple and then the other. Back and forth, until she was writhing beneath him. She lifted her hips, making contact with his engorged cock. He growled around her nipple and thrust his cock against her. She clawed at his back, loving the feel of touching him, of him touching her. On a groan, he leaned away and reached for his jeans, pulling out a condom and rolling it on in record time. When he hovered over her again, she rubbed her pussy against his hard length, aligning him at her entrance. He flexed his hips on impulse, and she gasped as he breached her.

He pulled his mouth away from the breasts he was ravishing and stared down at her, his swollen lips inches from hers. Their gazes locked and he pushed in farther, thrusting slowly. The look in his eyes almost undid her. They were so full of emotion she almost believed he did love her. But she wouldn't get her hopes up. She had to be smart about this, try to detach herself from her feelings.

He thrust hard, his eyes narrowing as he grabbed her hip and angled her for deeper penetration. "What are you thinking?" His next thrust was even harder than the last and she cried out at the pleasure. He kissed her ear. "Something sad crossed your eyes."

She shook her head, not wanting to voice her thoughts. She slid her hands down his back and squeezed his ass as she shoved her hips up, grinding into him. He groaned, his question clearly forgotten, and drove into her with maddening force.

"Oh God, Ian!"

"You feel so good, baby." His mouth was everywhere he could reach. Her throat, her breasts, her ears, her lips, kissing her urgently while she clutched him as tightly as she could. "Cassie, I love you."

No. She didn't want to think about that. She shook her head and held her breath, not even letting air in her lungs for fear his soul would find its way into her heart.

He slowed and looked at her, caressing her face. "You don't believe me?" he asked, hurt crossing his eyes.

"I don't want to think about that."

He nodded, resolved. "I want a chance to prove it to you. I know I'll have to earn your trust again, but baby, please know that I'll never do anything to hurt you ever again."

Her breath caught and tears formed, leaking over. Everything just seemed so hopeful, yet hopeless. Ian kissed them away as he gently started thrusting again. The frantic urgency subsiding, he made love to her slowly, reverently, whispering how beautiful she was and how sorry he felt for hurting her. They held each other tightly as they kissed and climbed toward that precipice together.

When Cassie went over, screaming his name, Ian kissed her hard, his hand sliding down to gently collar her throat. It was a mark of possession, and she found it extremely erotic, dragging out her orgasm as he thrust harder into her, shouting his own release.

As they both came down, he stroked her hair, kissed her lips, and she clung to him, not wanting to let him go.

"I do love you, Cassie. I want you to be mine again. Forever."

She was overwhelmed by the emotions rushing through her. But in a good way. She no longer wanted to hold back. "I-I love you too, Ian. That's why this has been so hard."

She felt his muscles relax at her admission, and he nodded his head against hers. "Never again. I'll never hurt you again. I'll show you I can deserve your love, baby."

He kissed her before rolling over and pulling her against him, stroking her hair. She sat quietly, wondering what would happen now. They loved each other but lived in different states. She guessed they could go back to their digital romance and get together on weekends, but that didn't sound very appealing after having felt his touch.

"They fired Mac," Ian murmured, playing with her locks.

"Oh yeah?" She wondered how many more would be on the chopping block during this restructuring.

"Mm-hmm. After he threatened to fire me if I said anything to the executive staff about what happened, I decided I could play just as dirty as him. I went to Mr. Winthrop and told him that your help was instrumental in the changes to the application and that Mac didn't tell me he was going to keep that from them. I reiterated my idea that we keep several positions from the southern office open, and he agreed it was a good idea."

Cassie's brain was churning. "Y-You asked to keep some of the people onboard?"

"Yeah, baby. I did the plan according to how Mac wanted me to, and I agree that it makes financial sense to close your office, but I felt it was necessary to keep some personnel. Mac shot that idea down. But when I explained to Mr. Winthrop my plan, he was impressed. So impressed, in fact, that they fired Mac and offered me his job. Well, part of it anyway. They're splitting it up, separating the business management and project management duties into two positions."

She gasped and turned to face him. "Wow. Congratulations."

He leaned up and kissed her quickly. "Well, it wasn't as clean as that," he said, chuckling. "I pulled up all of Mac's mistakes and showed Mr. Winthrop how many jobs were botched by him where I had to come in and clean up."

She laughed. "Nice. I'd have just uprooted his plants."

"What?" He chuckled.

"Nothing." She shook her head. "So what happens now?"

"Well." He pulled her back down to his chest. "I want you to come work with me," he whispered. "They want me to handle the business aspects of the operation, so I'd like you to be in the project management position that was split off from Mac's old duties."

"What?" Cassie asked incredulously, looking at him.

He swallowed nervously. "I love you, baby. I know you have a life here, but I want you to make a life with me. We can take this as slowly as you want, but I already know I want to spend the rest of my life with you."

"You're giving me a job?" Okay, so he just poured his heart out and she jumped to the part about her not being unemployed any-more. *A girl has gotta eat.*

He nodded. "It's yours if you want it. I've already cleared it with the executive staff. And if you agree, you get to select the posi-tions we keep from your office." His lips twitched, fighting a smile. "Except for Sasha. She's not staying in her old position. I've al-ready asked that she be promoted to my old job."

Cassie gasped, covering her gaping mouth. Ian had gone to all this trouble to make things right while she was busy moping around her house. He did this for her because he wanted to be with her. She smiled. She really wanted to be with him too, and now it seemed she'd get to do that. Then she laughed, thinking about being able to keep working with Sasha.

"What's so funny?"

"Let's tell Sasha this was my idea. I owe her for making her spank me that night. This should clear that debt."

He nuzzled her neck. "Hmm, I can't wait for you to do something bad so I can tan that ass myself."

She giggled, squirming in his embrace. "Well, apparently I kissed a guy a couple of times last night. Does that count?" she asked playfully.

He pulled away, staring her down, a look of mock anger crossing his face. "You've been making out with some guy while I've been pining away for you?"

"In my defense, I was really drunk. And Sasha was the one who wanted me to fuck him, and oh my God, I'm going to shut up now," she said as she saw the playfulness leave his expression.

He grabbed her lightning fast and slung her over his knees. "I'm going to spank you until you remember who you belong to, baby."

She laughed as he started swatting her, which quickly turned into moans, which quickly turned into an afternoon of her surrendering herself to his possession.

There really was no doubt who she belonged to.

Sasha loaded the last of her bags in the Uber she'd called to take her to the airport.

California bound.

She couldn't believe she was leaving her southern roots for a big city, trading in supped-up trucks for charming cable cars. It was a scary thing.

It was a liberating thing.

No doubt about it, though, it was time for a change. When the opportunity presented itself, she seized it. Of course, it was that or the unemployment line, but she didn't need nudging. Her career was her life. It always had been, but after what happened with her ex, she could use a fresh start.

A reboot.

Sasha shivered at the thought of that horrible man as she climbed into the car. Some scars never disappeared, but that didn't mean she couldn't use a little help forgetting they were there. Yeah, the sooner she got settled into her new life the faster she could close the chapter on her old one.

She'd taken the first step by accepting the job. The next step would be finding a place to live. Cassie had told her a little too eagerly not to worry about it. Whatever that meant.

Oh, you know. Her friend had probably already found Sasha an apartment in a building filled with hot, single men. Cassie would be sorely disappointed if she thought Sasha was going to be busy playing the field. There would be none of that mess. Her field was off limits still. Like seriously. She'd walled that shit off brick by brick after Dwight, and it'd take a tornado to knock them down.

California didn't get tornados. It was the perfect place for her.

With each passing mile, she felt something she hadn't in months. Lighter. The tension she'd carried eased, if only slightly.

She had already decided there'd be no more hardcore men. Ever. That rule would never change. Not that anyone could crush her carefully crafted walls, but why chance it?

No, when she was ready, she'd find a meek little thing who wasn't controlling or demanding, or she wouldn't be with anyone at all.

She was okay with that, too.

"PLEASE, Sir. I-I can't take it anymore."

Aaron Cope looked down at his sub for the night and suppressed a sigh because he knew just how true Gabi's words were. He, too, felt as if he couldn't take it anymore. He loved being a Dom and thought he loved the idea of no commitments. He was known around the club as a hard ass who didn't put up with shit, which meant he usually had subs vying for his attention—a fact he generally reveled in. But he was quickly discovering that more often than not, he felt alone even when he was fucking a woman. A sub for a night wasn't a true possession... She was a distraction. Not that the feeling stopped him from exerting his dominance and engaging in hot sex with a willing sub. He wasn't crazy. But lately when it was over, he tended to feel unfulfilled on some level. He had hit a proverbial brick wall in his sex life. No more progression, no more discoveries.

He ground his teeth. Regardless of how he felt, there were rules, and he would not tolerate a disobedient sub, no matter how new to the lifestyle she might be ... or how tedious it was all feeling to him of late.

He stepped around the St. Andrew's cross she was strapped to and grabbed her chin, forcing her to look up at him. "Gabriella, you are not to speak until I ask you a question unless it is to use your safe word. Do you wish to use it?"

She squirmed, and fuck, looking at a beautiful woman bound and marked by him never failed to make him harder than steel, which made him both hot and irritated at the same time. Why couldn't he just embrace his lifestyle like he always had? Aaron clenched his jaw and fisted his hands. He had a fucking sub to discipline. He'd deal with his emotional shit later.

"I-I'm sorry, Sir."

"I asked you a question, Gabriella."

"No, no, Sir. I don't wish to use it."

Aaron nodded at Gabi and caressed her chin where he'd been holding it. "Very well. That's ten more for speaking out of turn. Count them off and thank me for them."

Aaron walked around and grabbed the flogger he'd been using. He took position behind her again and drew back, landing exactly where he'd aimed.

"One," she gasped. "Thank you, Sir, for disciplining this sub."

Before she'd finished the last word, he'd swatted her again, and again, until her punishment was complete and her ass was bright red. She was moaning and wiggling, obviously aching for him, and he was ready to put an end to her torture. His too, because no matter how he'd been feeling, he was still turned on and ready to fuck.

He was shirtless already, so he unbuttoned his leathers and donned a condom. Before plunging into her, he grabbed her hair, yanked her head back, and put his mouth at her ear. "Gabriella, you've done well tonight. I'm going to fuck you now."

He didn't wait for a response, not that he expected one. He hadn't asked her a question, and if she spoke out of turn again, she'd just be prolonging her sexual release. Oh, he'd whipped other subs before until they'd come without him ever fucking them, but Gabi hadn't let herself go completely, hadn't experienced that subspace of euphoria that'd allow her the ultimate gift of submission. Though he hoped she would in time. Maybe when she found a Dom she wanted permanently. In the meantime, he'd enjoy her tonight like he did many others, and let her go when their scene was over.

Maybe it was time for him to think about finding a permanent sub of his own. The thought of that scared him, though he'd never admit it to anyone. He loved being single—well, at least he *had* loved it.

He took her forcefully, holding her naked hips as he plowed into her from behind.

"Oh, god, Sir." Gabi moaned and writhed what little she could move, her pussy like a vise around him as she came. And soon enough, he was digging his forehead into her shoulder and coming into the condom. He could've prolonged it, made it last for hours more, but he was ready to be finished with her. With this. Whatever that meant.

He slowly pulled out, discarded the condom, and unbound her from the contraption that he'd so loved to use.

"You pleased me tonight, Gabriella."

"Thank you, Sir."

He gathered her into his arms and sat with her on his lap, coddling her like he did every sub after conducting a scene. It was important to make sure a submissive felt that connection with her Dom in order to help her—or him, as the case might be with others—feel grounded, appreciated, nurtured, protected after giving that gift of submission.

Aaron loved this life. He only wished it fulfilled him as it had before.

Fucking brick walls.

———

CONTINUE SASHA'S and Aaron's story in ***California Crush***, which is out now!

———

LIKE YOUR HOT alpha men with a side of danger? The Bang Shift Series is romantic suspense, featuring mercenaries, mechanics, and the mafia! Pssst...Mason makes an appearance in several books and even gets his own story in this series. Start this wild ride with book one, ***Brody***.

———

HEY, y'all!

Thank you for reading my book. :) If you enjoyed it, I'd be very grateful for a review. If you didn't like it, then share that, too... as long as your review is honest, that's all that matters.

And ice cream. Ice cream matters, too.

Want the latest scoop? Be sure to sign up for my Newsletter! I mean, it's not as yummy as ice cream, but nothing ever is.

XOXO,
Mandy

Mandy Harbin is a *USA Today* Bestselling author who loves creating stories that explore the complexities of everyday relationships...with some kissing thrown in. She is a Superstar Award recipient, Reader's Crown and Passionate Plume finalist, and has achieved Night Owl Reviews Top Pick distinction many times. She also writes young adult romance as M.W. Muse because teens like kissing, too.

After graduating college and working many years in technology, she threw caution to the wind and began studying writing at the UALR. Years of trashed manuscripts and rejections eventually led to contracts and representation. With over thirty books published, she now serves on the board of her local writing chapter.

Mandy lives in a small, Arkansas town with her husband and their bossy dog, enjoying her own happily ever after...with some kissing thrown in.

mandyharbin.com/newsletter
facebook.com/Author.MandyHarbin
instagram.com/mandy_harbin
bookbub.com/authors/mandy-harbin

www.ingramcontent.com/pod-product-compliance
Lightning Source LLC
Chambersburg PA
CBHW030636190726
48286CB00008B/2547